A new anthology c

j

The Stars Afire

In *Lost Letters and Christmas Lights*, Christmas in Rome isn't quite what Giovanni and Beatrice had in mind, until a set of misplaced letters leads them back to their library in the heart of Italy. Serafina Rossi wasn't expecting vampires for Christmas, but the thought of meeting the cantankerous and intriguing ally of her employers is more than she can resist.

Giovanni Vecchio has a headache, and Richard Montegu is it. In *Finding Richard*, Giovanni and Beatrice head east to New York City in order to take care of a little problem who's been spotted off-off-Broadway.

Giovanni and Beatrice return to Italy in *Desires of the Heart*. With their nephew growing older every year, Giovanni and Beatrice travel to Rome for the holidays, this time with a new vision for their future and the future of their family.

The Stars Afire is a short story and novella anthology in the Elemental Mysteries series by Elizabeth Hunter.

THE STARS AFIRE

An Elemental Mysteries Anthology

ELIZABETH HUNTER

PRAISE FOR ELIZABETH HUNTER

Elizabeth Hunter's books are delicious and addicting, like the best kind of chocolate. She hooked me from the first page, and her stories just keep getting better and better. Paranormal romance fans won't want to miss this exciting author!

—Thea Harrison, NYT best-selling author of the Elder Races

A Hidden Fire is saturated with mystery, intrigue, and romance... This book will make my paranormal romance top ten list of 2011.

—Better Read Than Dead

Elemental Mysteries turned into one of the best paranormal series I've read this year. It's sharp, elegant, clever, evenly paced without dragging its feet, and at the same time emotionally intense.

—Nocturnal Book Reviews

The Stars Afire

Copyright © 2018

Elizabeth Hunter

ISBN: 9781730794131

Cover: Damonza

Editor: Anne Victory

Proofreader: Linda, Victory Editing

Recurve Press LLC

PO Box 4034

Visalia, California

USA

ElizabethHunterWrites.com

❀ Created with Vellum

Doubt thou the stars are fire,
Doubt that the sun doth move.
Doubt truth to be a liar,
But never doubt I love.

—William Shakespeare

A NOT-SO-SPECIAL NIGHT

"So who was Saint Valentine anyway?"

Giovanni hummed a little, stirring the sauce that was simmering on the stove. "No one is certain. According to one of the most popular legends, he was a Roman priest who was beheaded for officiating marriages of Christians during the reign of Claudius the Second. It was illegal under Roman law for Christians to marry, so they had to act in secret, but Valentinus was found out, beaten with stones and clubs, then finally beheaded outside the walls of the city."

Ben frowned, staring at the pot with the same quiet focus as his uncle. "Wow. Romantic. That explains all the hearts and flowers."

Giovanni raised an eyebrow. "It does exhibit a certain romantic dedication despite the unfortunate end result."

"Sort of like this dinner you're making."

"The pasta did not turn out that badly."

Ben used a wooden spoon to poke at the mangled lump sitting in the strainer. "I don't think it's supposed to stick together like that, dude."

"It'll be better with sauce." Giovanni shoved his nephew's

hand back and covered the pasta protectively. "Do not call me dude. Besides, she doesn't eat much."

Ben shook his head sadly. "You're how old? And you look like an Italian supermodel. You should be better at this. Did you get her flowers at least?"

Giovanni huffed. "Beatrice doesn't like flowers. She would rather have a book."

The young man rolled his eyes with all the wisdom of his seventeen years. "Every woman likes flowers. Even if they *say* they don't, they do."

He tried not to laugh. Ben still had a lot to learn about women, though the girls all seemed very eager to give him a chance. "I have actually celebrated this holiday with my wife before, Ben. But thank you for your thoughtful input. What are you and Chloe doing tonight?"

"I made reservations at her favorite restaurant." The boy's chest puffed out. "And I bought her flowers. Not roses. Lilies, which are her favorite. And we're going to a club later."

Giovanni raised an eyebrow. "Oh?"

"Not one that serves alcohol," Ben muttered, clearly unhappy with the fact. "But a bunch of her friends will be there, so we're all going to hang out."

"Ah." Giovanni nodded, pleased that the boy was spending time with other humans. "Excellent. And I like Chloe; she seems like a clever girl."

Ben stared at the red sauce thoughtfully. "She may be too smart for me."

Giovanni smirked. Leave it to Ben to finally find a girl who could outsmart him. "That's good. She can teach you humility. Something which you are sadly lacking."

"Look who's talking." Ben snickered. "Who's keeping you humble, pretty boy?"

"Benjamin..." Giovanni's voice was a low warning, though he was trying not to laugh.

Ben lifted his hands, framing his uncle with them. "Come on, Gio. Blue Steel. Show me your best Blue Steel."

Calmly, Giovanni picked up a sizable chef's knife from the block, glanced at the wall behind the boy, then flung it toward his nephew.

Ben sucked in a breath when he felt the knife whoosh past him and stick in the wall at his back. "Okay, no more *Zoolander* jokes. Got it. Caspar's gonna be pissed you put a knife mark in the wall though."

"Go." He waved his nephew away as he turned off the sauce. "Beatrice is coming up the drive. Shoo. Have fun with Chloe. Be back before the sun is up."

"Can I borrow your Mustang?"

"Will it get you out of here faster?"

"Yes."

"Fine." Giovanni reached over and tossed the boy the keys from the hook on the kitchen wall. "Now go."

"Sweet!" Ben ran to the refrigerator and grabbed a box of flowers, then hightailed it out the door just as Beatrice was walking in. "Hi! Bye!" He dropped a kiss on top of his aunt's head, then disappeared.

"Wow!" She laughed. "Date with Chloe?"

"I let him use the Mustang."

"What a nice uncle you are..." She sidled next to him and wrapped an arm around his waist as he stood at the stovetop. "And what a nice husband you are too. You didn't have to fix dinner. Thanks!"

"Here, taste the sauce." He lifted a spoon to her lips and she blew on it a little before she stuck out her tongue. The edge of one fang peeked out as she tasted the red sauce. The sight held him transfixed. She closed her mouth, pursing her lips together, a bit of sauce still lingering on her lower lip.

"It's... Hmm, well, it's—"

"Let me." Swooping down, he licked at her lip, covering

her mouth with his as he grabbed Beatrice and lifted her to the counter. He let his hands drift from the curve of her hips, up her ribs, brushing the sides of her breasts as she let out a playful growl.

"Gio," she murmured, pulling her mouth away for a second. "The sauce is—"

"Awful." He dragged her mouth back to his. "Absolutely awful. I know. The pasta is worse."

She smiled as he kissed her. "Cooking is not your strong suit." Then she ran her hands down his back, reveling in the feel of the hard muscle under the grey T-shirt he'd pulled on at dusk. "Luckily you have many other talents."

"Mmmm." He licked at the tip of her tongue, teasing her with a rush of energy that caused a hiss of steam to rise from her neck. "Yes, I do."

"I'm not hungry anyway."

He pulled her closer, rubbing up against her as her breath hitched. "Not at all?"

"Not for food."

"How very fortunate."

Giovanni lost himself in her. He was surrounded by his mate. Her blood called to him. Her scent sang. Forget having a particular day to show how much he loved her. She was everything. Every night. Every moment. He felt her fangs tease along his collarbone. Her fingers were pulling the edge of his shirt up. Her legs—

"Who was throwing knives, and why wasn't I invited?"

He hadn't even registered the extra presence.

With a groan, Beatrice tore her mouth from his. "Hi, Tenzin. I have no idea. Gio, why is there a knife stuck in the wall, and do we need to get rid of a body?"

"Too many people live in our house," he muttered. "Far too many people."

Tenzin shrugged, clearly not bothered by his displeasure.

"I'm leaving for a while, so please feel free to have sex in the kitchen while I'm gone."

He heard Beatrice stifle a laugh. Giovanni said, "Where are you going?"

"To the mountains for a while. It's too loud here. I'll be back later."

For Tenzin, being back later could mean a week or two years. There was no way of knowing, so he only nodded and asked, "Anything we need to watch while you're gone?"

"No." Well, it wouldn't be years then. If that were the case, she'd probably ask Ben to water the plants at her warehouse. "Goodbye."

And with that, she was out the door.

Beatrice said, "Has she always been like that?"

"As long as I've known her." He helped Beatrice down from the counter and opened the fridge to grab a bottle of wine. "And I do have my finer moments, despite what my nephew thinks."

She cocked her head. "What's that?"

"This, my wife—" He set the bottle of wine down on the counter and grabbed her around the waist. He hummed a little tune as he turned Beatrice in the middle of the kitchen, dancing in the now-silent house. "This is the last bottle from a very special case of champagne."

She smiled and moved with him. "Oh?"

"You see, I once drank a bottle of this champagne with a beautiful girl on the night she graduated from university. I was the only one there to celebrate with her, and secretly I was glad. I was jealous of her attention, and I didn't want to share her."

A look of wonder spread over her face. "Really?"

"Mm-hmm." He nodded, continuing to move her in their silent dance. "Later, I went down to the wine cellar in an old house in Houston, and I took the rest of that case and set it aside. There were ten bottles left."

They continued to sway to the music only they could hear.

She asked in a quiet voice, "And what did you do with them?"

"I drank a bottle here and there for a few years." He tried not to shudder when he thought of the dark years he had spent away from her. "On nights when I especially missed her, I drank a bottle and remembered what it had been like to see her smile and laugh."

He saw red-tinged tears at the corners of her eyes as he bent down and kissed her again.

"Gio," she whispered against his lips.

"And then, when I finally saw her again—when she finally forgave me for leaving her—I took her to a play for our first date. And before we went, I opened another bottle and poured it for her, watching her eyes light up even though I hadn't told her it was the same wine."

Her awed expression turned into a smile. "In Santiago. That night."

"I opened another on the night she agreed to marry me," he said in a soft, urgent voice. "The night I knew she would be mine for eternity. I opened one then."

He had stopped moving as he stared at her, his breath halting as he took her in. Over five hundred years of jaded existence, wiped out by a love so strong and pure it made him question everything he had become cynical about. "And then there was one bottle left."

Her smile was soft, tremulous in the low light. "It's just Valentine's Day. What's so special about—"

"I don't need to be reminded of her smiles anymore," he said. "Because she gives them to me every night. When I wake, she is the first thing I see. When I dream, I hear her laugh. And so I don't need this reminder." He kissed her one more time before he reached for the bottle of wine. "Instead of flowers or elaborate dinners or grand gifts, I'll share the last bottle from that case with her, then I will make love to her for hours and fall into sleep with her in my arms. And that, *tesoro*, is all I need to be happy, on Valentine's night or any other night."

Beatrice grabbed the bottle from him and set it on the counter before she leapt into his arms. He caught her and held on.

"Wow," she said breathlessly, "you are really good at this."

He grinned and said, "I know."

Giovanni held her with one arm while he grabbed the bottle with the other. Beatrice snagged two champagne flutes from a cupboard before he walked toward the stairs.

"Happy Valentine's Day, Gio."

"Happy Valentine's Day, *tesoro*."

MERRY CHRISTMAS, TENZIN

"Scrooge."

"If you are referring to the literary character, I do not think the reference is apt."

Ben set down the sports section and rolled his eyes. "I was referring to the popular concept of someone who refuses to celebrate a holiday."

"For the last time, I am not a Christian. This is a holiday to celebrate the incarnation of the Christian god and his human journey." Tenzin shrugged and continued to fiddle with whatever she was making on the stove. "An admirable celebration, but not one that I choose to take part in."

"It's about more than the religious celebration, Tiny."

"I really dislike that nickname."

"And yet"—Ben grinned and took a sip of coffee—"I will call you that anyway."

"And I will hit you even harder the next time we fight." She looked up from the stove where a delicious aroma was starting to drift to Ben's nose. Tenzin didn't cook often, but when she did, everyone showed up and he barely got any. She wasn't very good at estimating portion sizes. When Tenzin cooked, she got out one of the old cooking pots she kept in Caspar's kitchen, threw random things in, and in short order, the house smelled amazing.

That night Caspar and Isadora were gone, spending the weekend with Ernesto on the yacht, Giovanni and Beatrice were out hunting, and Ben was stuck at home. It was winter break, so his college classes were out, and he was bored. Luckily, he had Tenzin to pick on and no one to share the food with. All in all, not a bad night.

"Why are you here?" she asked, stirring whatever spicy, delicious thing she was making. "Shouldn't you be out with your friends, making Gio worry?"

"I'm installing that voice-recognition software on the computers tonight." *And eating your food.*

"And eating my *dapanji.*"

Am I old enough to know what that means? Ben stifled a smile and finished his coffee before he stood and walked to the kitchen. "What's dapanji?"

"This dish I'm making." She looked up at him, then scowled at the coffee cup in his hand. "No more coffee. Drink tea. You drink too much coffee."

Ben put his coffee cup in the sink and reached for the small pot of fragrant tea next to the stove. She'd set out two mugs. "Yes, all that coffee has obviously stunted my growth."

"So, so proud of sheer verticality, Benjamin." She whipped a small foot back, aiming a quick kick at the back of his leg that almost caused him to fall over. "Makes you easier to take down."

"Hey, no fighting in the kitchen." Ben caught himself on the edge of the counter. Hot tea splashed his hand. "Caspar will get mad."

"At you."

"He gets mad at you too. He just can't do anything about it." Ben decided to abandon the newspaper and keep her company, so he hopped up on the counter to irritate her about his favorite subject of the moment.

"You know...," he started again as she lifted the edge of the lid. He caught a glimpse of some spicy-looking red broth before the lid fell. "There are all sorts of winter holidays you could choose from. Christmas, Yule, Hanukkah, Kwanzaa. What did you celebrate as a human?"

"Survival."

"I'm serious, Tenzin."

"So am I." She turned and poured herself a cup of tea. "Fine, we celebrated agricultural holidays. Harvest. Spring. The summer solstice. Things like that."

He grinned at her unexpected answer. "Were there gifts?"

"No, there was food." She gave Ben a reluctant smile. "That was gift enough."

"Well, I think you should celebrate Christmas with us. Just to fit in."

"But I do not fit in." She shrugged and sipped her tea, the curling fangs evident behind her lips. Unlike most vampires, Tenzin's fangs never retracted. They were frozen in vicious readiness at all times. And instead of the long, straight canines that most immortals had, Tenzin's had a distinctive curve that reminded Ben of the saber she usually fought with. It was one of the reasons she rarely smiled in public. Anything more than a murmur in front of humans made hiding what she was very difficult.

"You fit in here," he said, his voice suddenly soft.

She looked up at him. Those eyes. He had to force himself to meet them. Those eerie grey eyes saw... everything.

"Fine. I'll celebrate Christmas with all of you. But I'm not singing."

Ben grinned. "Cool. So what are you getting me?"

Her mouth dropped. "I never agreed to gifts!"

"Yes, you did. That's half of what Christmas is about." He

snickered and poured himself another cup of tea. "I know what I'm getting you."

She cocked her head to the side. "You're getting me a gift?"

"Yep. Already have it picked out."

"So this whole insistence that I celebrate a Christian holiday was so you could give me a gift?"

"Kind of. But not entirely." He reached over and patted the top of her head. "Come on, you'll have fun. There's food and drink and presents under the tree. Everyone will be here. We'll watch Christmas movies later."

"Which movies? There are very few action movies set on Christmas. I'm not watching anything with talking animals."

He shrugged. "*Home Alone?*"

"I do like the resourcefulness of that child. Kevin would make an excellent vampire."

Just then he heard two sets of footsteps outside. "Aw, man, are Gio and B back?"

Tenzin nodded. She would have heard them long before Ben did. "Yes, but they smell like they've both just eaten, so they shouldn't pig too much of your food."

"'Hog,' Tiny. 'Hog' the food."

"It's a stupid expression."

The door opened and a rush of cool air wafted in. Winter in Southern California was never all that cold, but they'd had a few storms come through in the past week, so the air was crisp and surprisingly chilly.

Giovanni said, "What's a stupid expression?"

"'Hogging' food," Tenzin said. "It's a stupid expression."

Giovanni shrugged. "Have you seen pigs eat? Not all that different from Ben."

"Hey!"

Beatrice slipped through the kitchen door. "Tenzin, that smells amazing. What is it?"

"Dapanji. It's a kind of stew with chicken and garlic and chilies."

"It smells divine. I'd love a taste."

Ben shook his head. "No. I had plans! You were all supposed to be gone. The Tenzin food is mine."

Giovanni sniffed the air, which was suddenly alive with the energy of three powerful vampires crowded into a small space. "Did you make naan?"

"You don't get the naan!"

Tenzin nodded. "It's in the oven. It's the kind with sesame seeds on it."

Beatrice came over and patted Ben's cheek. Her fingers were ice-cold. "Don't worry. We won't eat much. We're pretty full."

He didn't shiver. Not much, anyway, but her fangs were still down and her eyes were bright and his favorite aunt was looking particularly vampire-like dressed completely in black. Ben swallowed the instinctive lump in his throat that often came when you were the only one with an active pulse in a room full of creatures who drank blood for dinner.

"It's fine. I can share."

Beatrice grinned. There was slight smear of blood at the corner of her mouth.

"Uh, B... you might want to..." Ben mimed wiping the corner of his mouth.

"Oh!" She caught on and grabbed a napkin from a drawer. "That's embarrassing."

Giovanni bent down and whispered something in her ear that made Beatrice laugh, and suddenly it was just home again. Giovanni and Tenzin started chatting in Chinese, and Beatrice began teasing Ben about two of the girls he was dating from school.

"Oh hey," he said, finally interrupting her. "I got Tenzin to agree to celebrate Christmas with us."

"Yay!" Beatrice clapped her hands. "I know what I'm getting her already."

"If you just wanted to buy me things"—Tenzin took the steaming dish to the table where Giovanni was putting out four large bowls—"you don't have to make up an excuse. I accept gifts at all times."

Ben said, "But it's more fun when they're wrapped up under the Christmas tree and you know they're there, but you can't open them."

She curled her lip. "I have to wait?"

Ben and Beatrice nodded in tandem. "Yep," he said. "For *weeks*."

She growled a little. "I do not like that."

Beatrice grabbed the warm bread from the oven. "Why do I think that's part of the appeal for the boy?"

"The boy" watched her take the bread to the table and stand on her toes to give her husband a kiss as he poured four small glasses of golden beer.

She looks the same.

She always would. Though Ben was growing and changing, losing the softer angles of childhood and growing stronger and sharper every day, Beatrice stayed the same. Tenzin stayed the same. They all did. It wasn't something he'd thought about much as a child, when being a grown-up seemed so very far away, but the older he got, the more evident it became.

Sometimes he would go to Dez and Matt's house for a few days. He'd eat breakfast out on their patio in the sun and play with little Carina, who chattered in her adorable toddler-speak and seemed to change every day. Once, after Caspar had an unexpected problem with his heart, Ben had stayed with Matt and Dez for almost a month. They hadn't asked why, and neither had Giovanni or Beatrice.

But he came back. He imagined he always would.

"So, Ben, what are you getting me for Christmas?" Giovanni asked as he spooned an entirely too generous portion of the savory stew into his bowl. Ben watched him carefully before he grabbed the ladle and served himself.

"I don't know. I was thinking about an iPad."

"Ha ha," Giovanni said. Ben was still sore that his uncle had shorted out his last two electronic devices when he'd forgotten them in the library. "Don't leave them lying around and they'll survive longer. Or stick with paper books."

"E-books are the wave of the future, old man." Ben grabbed two large pieces of naan.

Giovanni shuddered visibly, then turned to his wife. "What about you? What are you getting me?"

"Do you really want me to say at the table?"

Giovanni grinned as Ben groaned and said, "No. None of us want that."

Tenzin muttered, "Like rabbits, those two."

"I know. Tiny, this is amazing, as usual."

"Thank you. Don't call me Tiny. What are you getting me for this holiday you convinced me to celebrate for purely selfish purposes?"

"I'm not telling you. Trust me, you'll like it."

"Is it sharp or poisonous? Because I like things like that."

Ben grinned. "I know. And I'm not even giving you a hint." The twin daggers Baojia had found for him would be perfect. They were ceremonial pieces that had drained much of his substantial bank account, but he knew exactly where she would hang them in her studio. "You'll have to be patient. B, I'm still stuck on what to get the old man here."

"What do you get for the five-hundred-year-old fire vampire who has everything? I struggle with that one myself." Beatrice shrugged. "Books. If all else fails, books."

Giovanni smiled. "I don't mind being predictable. And I already have your present, *tesoro*."

"You mean the Kimber Solo nine millimeter?"

His spoon dropped to the bowl. "How—"

"You wouldn't let me buy it at the shop. You insisted I'd like the Sig Sauer more, even though you know I like Kimbers." She tore off a piece of her naan. "It was kind of obvious, Gio."

Giovanni scowled and took another piece of bread. "You don't know about the other thing though."

"Is it a first edition of some book I love?"

He cleared his throat. "Maybe."

"You really are predictable," Tenzin muttered. "This food is excellent. I am still a very good cook."

"Yes, you are," Beatrice said. "Thanks, Tenzin."

"You should cook something for Christmas dinner," Ben said. "What do they eat in China for Christmas?"

"Noodles. Or dumplings. Or whatever you eat on Tuesday, because they don't celebrate Christmas."

Beatrice said, "Some people might now. Young people?"

"It's ironic when you think about it," Giovanni mused. "Most Christmas decorations are probably made in China."

"All those tinsel trees?" Ben said. "They must think Americans are seriously weird people."

"Americans *are* seriously weird people." Tenzin suddenly brightened. "If I'm celebrating Christmas, can we have fireworks?"

Giovanni said, "I'm fairly sure that's illegal."

"I don't even know where we'd find them," Beatrice added.

"Yes." Ben had everyone's attention. "I'll find them somewhere, and Gio—" He turned to his uncle. "If the cops show up, you can make them think all they heard was champagne bottles popping. Tiny wants fireworks; she gets fireworks."

Tenzin clapped as Beatrice smiled at Ben.

He just shrugged like it was no big deal. "But you have to cook."

"I will make the noodles you like."

Ben tried to act cool. "Score one for me. I'm not sharing."

He glanced up at Tenzin, who was smiling like a little kid, her fangs sparkling in the light from the kitchen, her eyes lit up. She totally didn't have to make the noodles; her expression alone was enough. Still, he wasn't going to turn them down.

"Merry Christmas, Tenzin."

LOST LETTERS AND CHRISTMAS LIGHTS

Serafina Rossi wasn't expecting vampires for Christmas. But as the director of the Vecchio Library, she can't refuse to help. And if part of that help is spending the holiday in Rome examining mysterious letters at the Vatican... Well, she can't exactly refuse.

Zeno Ferrara is an immortal whose eternity is dedicated to examining historical correspondence. But it's letters from the lovely director of the Vecchio Library that occupy his thoughts. Two years of correspondence have made Fina Rossi more than a mystery to be discovered. She's become his fascination.

When Fina shows up at Zeno's library just before Christmas, will they both discover an unexpected gift? And will a centuries-old mystery finally be resolved as Giovanni and Beatrice track down a clandestine romance hidden by history?

PROLOGUE

Los Angeles, California

"Beatrice?" Giovanni raised his voice only slightly when he entered the house,in San Marino knowing that despite its massive square footage, his mate would be able to hear him.

There was no response.

He pulled off the scarf he'd wrapped around his neck when he'd left earlier that evening. The weather in Southern California was mildly cool that December, which meant every native Californian had broken out their warmest wraps. It was so hard following winter fashion when there simply was no winter. Nevertheless, the humans tried.

"Beatrice?" he called again, wondering if she'd left the house. He reached out with his senses.

A hint of chicken *mole* in the air. Caspar had cooked it yesterday.

Doyle, his grey cat, purred near a fire someone had lit in the downstairs sitting room.

No sign of Ben, but that was hardly remarkable this time of night.

He inhaled again.

Vanilla. Acid. Almonds. And a very faint waft of mold.

Giovanni smiled. Beatrice was in the library.

The unmistakable trace of her amnis permeated the air. She'd been in the kitchen recently. Other immortals wouldn't sense it, but Beatrice De Novo wasn't only his wife by human law, she was his vampire mate by tradition. The blood they shared bound them on an elemental level. He always knew when she was near.

Her preternatural senses would have picked up the smallest sound, which meant she was ignoring him. Ignoring him meant one of two things. He calmly walked up the stairs to the second floor, stroking a finger along the side of the Vietnamese vase she'd found for him in Hong Kong the Christmas before.

Beatrice ignoring his call meant she was feeling playful or...

He nudged open the door to the library, leaning against it as he watched her muttering over a table piled with file boxes.

She was in the middle of a project.

"*Ciao bella, tesoro.*"

She waved one hand, which was covered in a silk glove because she was handling documents. She didn't lift her head. "Hey. Why are you..." Her mind drifted off before she could finish the question.

"Back so soon?" Giovanni finished for her. "The client wanted the impossible. I refuse to break something out of the National Archives."

"You have before."

"There were multiple copies of that *particular* item." He stepped closer, careful not to touch any of the materials spread over the table. "This item is unique. I'm not interested in depriving a nation of its history—meager though it may be —to satisfy a vampire's whim."

"So kind of you," she muttered, not even rising to the American history taunt. She'd continued her personal research project of documenting daily life in the mission period of California history that she'd started in graduate school. Giovanni had continued to acquire difficult-to-obtain books and documents for his immortal clientele and discreet human collectors. Beatrice helped him when it suited her, and both kept as busy as they wanted.

It was a good life. Others might think Giovanni longed for the excitement of his nights as an assassin or was jealous of the power others wielded in vampire politics. Power he had handed to them before he stepped away.

But Giovanni Vecchio had no longing for violence. No desire for power. He had spent hundreds of years with both thrust upon him. Now he had found his peace.

He and his mate flew around the world as they liked, visiting their homes and perusing their books. Working when they wanted. Keeping in touch with friends and occasionally assisting with a problem when help was requested.

But, for the most part, they lived a quiet life.

"How's the new pub?" She had put down the letter she'd been examining, sliding the acid-free envelope into the file before she pulled out another. "Ben says Gavin's happy as a clam in New York. He's considering making the move permanent. Keeps making noises about the O'Briens, but nothing serious."

"Gavin would gripe about Mother Teresa if he'd spent any time with her. The O'Briens aren't causing him any trouble. And I don't like the manager of Gavin's pub. I miss the one in Houston."

"That's too bad."

"We should go back for a visit."

"To the pub?"

He laughed a little. "To Houston. We could make a visit of it. See Gavin. Charlotte. Maybe Claire and Andor."

"Uh-huh."

He sat down and leaned his head in his hand. "We could break into the Rothko Chapel. Finally steal the black canvases you like."

"Yeah... sounds good," she responded, clearly not paying attention. Beatrice was occupied with the letter she held.

It looked like part of the mission correspondence she'd been collecting.

"What is it?" he asked, giving up on discussing anything other than work.

"Remember the Hungarian you shoved in my direction?"

"The wine collector?"

"Wine*maker*," she said, correcting him. "Rabidly private. Old. I think I may have a lead on that project."

"I thought you'd given up on it."

"No. Put it on the back burner for a bit, but he was getting rude."

Giovanni's head came up. "Explain rude."

Beatrice smiled as he stood and walked to the table. "Nothing I can't handle, handsome. I told him to back off, but then I ran across something when I was helping one of Katya's archivists. There was a mention in a letter from Father Ignacio..."

She trailed off again, but Giovanni started paging through the box of letters, each one a carefully preserved missive from one of the Franciscan priests or secular clergy at California's twenty-one original missions. Over the years, Beatrice had come to know many of the more prolific letter writers by name. Father Ignacio was a favorite.

"He mentions a young priest around San Jose who was an expert in winemaking and had begun sending out '*un informe*.'

I think I have some letters that priest exchanged with another in Rome. Odd, I thought at the time, because why Rome? Why not Spain?"

"If he was a member of the clergy, it's possible he—"

"Had connections with someone in the church there. I figure that's why. Anyway, I'd misread '*informe*' as a verb, not a noun. But *un informe* would be a... report. An account of some kind. Something written down. At least that's what the context would imply from what I remember."

He paid half a mind to what she was saying and the other half to the excitement in her voice. The animated way her eyes lit up as she tugged the thread of history hidden within the papers before her.

It was almost ridiculous how he loved her.

"So if this priest was writing down his practices and sending them to his contemporaries in the other missions, it might not be just a report, but maybe a journal? A book? Which is exactly what the Hungarian wants and I thought didn't exist. But now I think it does! I just need to find out how many copies he made of this thing and pray one survived. If I can figure out where he sent them... I'm hoping there's something in the letters to Rome that will give me some more to go on."

Giovanni pursed his lips when he realized what letters she was referring to. "The letters? The... Roman ones? Written from the Vatican?"

"Yes." She closed one box and opened another. "Well, they were written in Rome but were sent to a California Franciscan. So they should be in here. All my mission correspondence—I just... can't..." She sighed. "This is driving me crazy. I've been looking for hours."

It really was too bad that he hadn't skipped the meeting with the impossible vampire and come home hours ago. "My love, I think I know the letters you're speaking of."

"I know!" Beatrice threw up her hands, and they landed on her hips. "I remember cataloguing them last fall. They should be in this box, but they aren't."

"Well..."

"Gio?" She must have caught the look on his face. "What did you do with my letters?"

"They were written from Rome."

Her eyes narrowed. "Yes, but they were written to a priest in *California*. Clearly they needed to be with the mission letters."

"One could argue"—he cleared his throat—"that they were more properly filed with Vatican correspondence. Since they were written *from* the Vatican."

Beatrice's mouth dropped open. "You did not."

He shrugged. "You were in the middle of some research with Lucien, and I was having a number of things transferred to the Perugian library, so—"

"Gio, you didn't!" Her hands gripped her hair. "You sent my letters to Fina?"

The library that Giovanni's deceased son had established in Perugia had continued to be run by Serafina Rossi, the human Lorenzo hired to curate the collection in his absence. She truly was a very competent human who had proven to be trustworthy despite having been chosen by his scheming son. Gradually, Giovanni and Beatrice had enlightened Fina and her son, Enzo, about the immortal world they'd been dragged into unawares. Both had come under Giovanni's protection, and he did not take the responsibility lightly. Plus Fina was a superb archivist with a background in art history.

"The Perugia library has far more room than this one, *tesoro*. And you know I've been transferring materials there when they fit the collection—"

"But they're not Vatican letters! They're mission letters! I cannot believe you lost my materials—"

He drew up, slightly offended. "I did not 'lose' them. They remain catalogued here, and I put a notation in the files that they were being stored in Perugia with the Vatican papers there."

Slightly mollified, Beatrice stopped yelling, but her angry expression did not wane. "You took *mission* letters."

"I took Vatican letters."

"Sent to a mission. *My* mission."

He bit back a laugh. "I do not believe you have a greater claim than the church, my love."

"And I know there's a reference in those letters to this journal or book about winemaking that the Hungarian wants. And it's all the way in Perugia! And I can't ask Fina to dig through all that stuff—"

"There is no 'digging' necessary." He felt his skin heat in anger. "Beatrice, you're acting as if I threw them in a cardboard box and tossed them in a suitcase. I would never—"

"You're right." Her expression softened. "You're right. That was out of line. You would never treat original documents that way."

"Thank you." He was still a bit put out. To think she'd accuse him of being that careless...

"Well," she said. "There's really only one thing to do."

"What?"

Her frown turned to an impish grin. "Clearly we're spending Christmas in Italy this year."

Christmas in Italy? Away from both their families and all their employees?

Giovanni tugged Beatrice to him, and her silk-covered hands came up to brush his cheeks as he took her mouth in a lingering kiss.

"What a truly"—he nipped Beatrice's lips and pulled her toward the low couches at one end of the room—"*truly* excellent idea."

"I know." She grabbed his perfectly pressed dress shirt and tore the buttons off as she pulled it open. "I'm brilliant that way."

His fangs dropped as he licked up her neck, murmuring, "*Buon natale* to me."

"Wait!" She pulled away from his kiss. "Is Italy one of those countries that doesn't exchange presents until January?"

"Yes, January 6h. The Epiphany."

"No!"

"You'll survive. Now kiss me."

CHAPTER 1

Citta di Castello
Perugia, Italy

Serafina Rossi carefully sorted the letters her employers had asked her to find from within the mass of correspondence recently added to the Vecchio Library. Though she understood Dr. Vecchio's reasons, she had to agree with Ms. De Novo's somewhat frantic email. The letters, despite being written from Rome, appeared to belong within the De Novo Library in Los Angeles, which specialized in early Californian —particularly Spanish-era—history.

Fina walked around the massive library tables that occupied the floor in the central quadrangle of bookcases. Soft lights illuminated the letters from discreetly hidden sources in the walls of the villa. She reached a long arm to straighten two of the letters, nudging them into a perfect line in chronological order.

Everything was ready for her employers' arrival, and she'd taken a short nap that afternoon in preparation for a late evening, as she always did when Dr. Vecchio or Ms. De Novo was in residence. They stayed in the villa if they needed to use the library for research. She knew they had an estate near Florence, but they preferred to stay in the convenient rooms her former employer had renovated on the second floor.

What they needed the California letters for, she had no idea. But she was a librarian. Her task was to conserve and organize the information, not ask questions.

Written by a young, well-connected Franciscan in Rome, the documents Ms. De Novo had requested were addressed to "my dear friend, Brother Rafael of Mission San Jose" in California. The first were dated in 1798 and the last in 1803. Five years of the earliest correspondence in mission-era California. They were... not terribly interesting, in Fina's opinion. Speaking mostly of church matters, the earliest were written in a familiar tone. She hadn't had time to read them all yet. The most curious thing was the identity of the writer. "Father P——" was the only designation given.

There were inquiries about the establishment of the mission. A few mentions of holidays, university classes, and mutual acquaintances with very prominent names. These Franciscans were far from country brothers, which made the assignment of the Spanish priest to the California missions rather unusual.

Yes, definitely materials better sorted out in the De Novo Library.

But it was not Fina's job to decide these things. In the two years she'd worked for the Vecchio-De Novo family, she had experienced far more than the usual quirks her colleagues at private libraries reported.

But then, as far as she knew, their employers were entirely human.

"Mama!" Her son, Enzo, called from the front garden. "I think I see the car!"

The winter sun had fallen several hours before, and Enzo was looking forward to their company.

It was a quiet life she and her son lived in Perugia, which did not bother Fina, though the country was beginning to chafe at Enzo, twelve years old and the center of her universe.

Enzo, books, and the odd request from vampire employers. It wasn't the life she'd thought she'd be living twelve years ago when she finished her time at university, but it had given her independence when her family had shunned her. She was from a small town outside Venice, and though her parents paid lip service to sophistication, the reality of an unwed daughter expecting a baby made them balk.

Only her grandmother had remained in contact after Enzo was born. And she'd lost her *nonna* when her son was only five.

It was losing Nonna that had hurt the most. Fina had always been a quiet child. It was Nonna who had encouraged her to follow her dreams.

"Fina, dreams will not come to you. You must go out and chase them."

She'd chased them all the way to university before she'd been swept off her feet and into her professor's bed. His scoffing rejection of her and the baby they'd created had caused her to retreat.

In her heart, she knew Nonna would be disappointed. But Fina lived for Enzo now. His happiness and security were far more important than her own.

She felt far older than thirty-eight years. She lived alone and didn't fit with the friendly, domestic mothers in the village where her son went to school. Yet rarely could she leave the library that had been her responsibility for twelve years to go to professional conferences or gatherings of her peers. Not only was she a single mother, but the Vecchio

ELIZABETH HUNTER

Library was her creation. Other than Enzo, its organization was her greatest achievement.

She supposed few would understand that.

Another set of letters caught her eye, tucked into the front pocket of the briefcase on the edge of the table and filed in a manila envelope. Those letters were not written by an eighteenth-century Franciscan but a somewhat mysterious colleague at the Vatican Library in Rome.

She'd never met Zeno Ferrara, but the former priest turned immortal had been introduced to her—via hand-written letter, of course—by Dr. Vecchio. In the past two years, Ferrara had offered her a wealth of information regarding anything to do with church history. And though Ferrara was no longer a priest, he still worked at the Vatican Library in some unknown capacity.

They had never met. But through the odd intimacy of their correspondence, Fina had begun to wish that they could.

It was silly, she supposed.

And yet the often terse letters Ferrara sent had lately shown evidence of... something.

"My dear Signora Rossi, I wonder whether I should be flattered or annoyed by your persistence. Are you always this forward?"

Forward? If she was forward, he was the only one who had ever implied it. The irritating man had put off her question about Pope Alexander VI for over three weeks. When he finally did answer, his letter was so thorough it could have been submitted to an academic journal.

"...I wonder if I should be flattered or annoyed...?"

Flattered? The implication brought a hint of the furious blush to her cheeks that had plagued her since childhood.

"Surely a young woman has better ways of spending a weekend than organizing papal correspondence. Or are the charms of Perugia such that you seek excitement from church relics?"

Well, really.

What kind of man became a priest and then a vampire anyway? Did he look like the priests she'd grown up with, paternal men with cheerful faces and kind eyes? Or would he look like the vampires she'd met when Dr. Vecchio or Ms. De Novo had brought visitors? Beautiful—almost all the vampires she'd met were beautiful—but remote. Cold. Her employers seemed to be exceptions to the rule. From the wry humor that slipped through Signor Ferrara's letters, she thought Signor Ferrara might be too. Their letters had begun professionally but became familiar. Past his quips, Fina could see that Zeno Ferrara had a passion for his work that she could appreciate.

What would he look like?

She couldn't imagine. And, she supposed, it was better that she didn't. Ferrara was a colleague. It behooved her to remain aloof should they ever meet. Daydreaming about what the vampire's eyes might look like was a childish distraction.

She heard the car doors slam shut, then Enzo began shouting in rapid Italian despite the English she'd so carefully tutored him in.

"Dr. Vecchio, this car is—"

"Please, Enzo." A laughing voice interrupted her son. "You must call me Giovanni. How many times have I asked now?"

"My mother would not want me to be so informal, signore."

"*Signor* Giovanni then," a woman's voice suggested. "And Signora Beatrice for me."

"If you like," Enzo said politely just as Fina reached the door.

"*Dottore*, signora." She held out a hand as their driver stowed the car and himself... somewhere. There was always a near-invisible human servant or driver escorting the Vecchio-De Novos everywhere they went. They didn't carry phones or briefcases; the driver did. Fina had almost become accustomed to it. "Welcome," she said. "It is so good to see you."

"Please, Fina," Beatrice pled with her. "Please call me Beatrice. There is no need to be so formal."

Fina hesitated. She'd allowed herself to become familiar with her former employer—going so far as to consider Paulo a friend—only to discover after he had died that he was not a good man at all, but rather a vicious monster who had killed many, including Beatrice's own father. Only for Serafina and Enzo had he redeemed himself. Paulo—*Lorenzo*—had reserved all his humanity for them.

She didn't know why. She would never understand. But she had learned caution. Things were not always what they appeared to be in the vampire world.

But if her employers wished her to be more familiar, she would be.

"Of course," she said with a smile. "Beatrice. Giovanni. How are you both?"

"Well, thank you," Giovanni replied. "As always, we appreciate your accommodating us."

"Of course. Signora Giannini has prepared the upstairs rooms for you if you'll be staying here."

"We will be," Beatrice said. "Thanks, Fina." Beatrice's eyes lit up. "Now, let's see those letters."

Fina saw Enzo's face fall just a little. He masked it quickly.

But not so quickly for Giovanni not to have caught it.

"I'd love to stretch my legs a bit," he said, kissing Beatrice with easy affection. "Why don't you and Fina start, and maybe I could trouble Enzo to kick a ball with me for a bit."

"Yes, of course," the boy exclaimed. "Let me go to the house."

Fina glanced down at Dr. Vecchio's impeccably polished shoes. "Dottore—"

"Again," he said, "please call me Giovanni. And I am happy to play a bit of football with your son if he is willing to indulge me." He winked at her. "My nephew is too busy for me these days. And Enzo is a good boy."

Fina's heart melted. "Of course. He is very excited to have you both visit."

Beatrice smiled. "We've been looking forward to seeing him too." She hooked Fina's arm with hers. "Now, let's leave the boys to their games and go look at my letters."

☙❧

"SHE'S SO LONELY," BEATRICE SAID LATER THAT NIGHT after she and Giovanni had locked themselves in the secure, lightproof room on the second floor of the library. Rudy, the young valet Caspar was training, had taken the small room off the garage.

"Who?" He frowned, looking up from the book he'd been reading. "Serafina?"

"Mm-hmm." Beatrice pulled her earrings off and set them on the dresser in the lavish suite Lorenzo had designed. They hadn't had time to redecorate it, but it wasn't as ostentatious as most of Giovanni's late son's holdings. "I think she works too much. This library is her life."

Giovanni frowned as if he didn't quite understand why that was a problem.

Her husband. Five hundred years old and still somewhat clueless about the female of the species.

"So what is it that you want to do?" he asked. "Move the library? We cannot do that. I mean, we could, but it would be horribly wasteful. Lorenzo may have been a monster, but this facility..."

It was the one thing that his son had ever done right. Possibly the only humanity Lorenzo had retained. And she knew it was one of the reasons Giovanni liked to be here. Maybe why he hadn't changed a thing. Not even their room.

"I don't want to move the library," she said. "The library is perfect." The slight tension in his shoulders disappeared. "And I think Fina likes to be here. She's a quiet person. But maybe we should make an effort to see that she leaves occasionally. Think about it, Gio."

"She's isolated here." He nodded. "Yes, I can see that."

"She's estranged from her family. She and her son occupy that weird between place of living in both the vampire world and the human one. It's not like she's in LA where Enzo could go to Ben's school and be around other day people's children. Whom does she confide in? Where does she vent?"

Giovanni said, "I hadn't thought of that. But you're correct. If I think about our human employees at home, they mostly socialize with us or other vampire employees. There is a community there. Here, there is none."

"Matt and Dez. My grandma and Caspar. Rudy has already become friendly with everyone. Fina has no one here. If she were closer to Rome..." Beatrice shrugged.

"It's not even three hours by car. She could visit there if she liked. Even use the house in town. Angela would love it."

Beatrice smiled. "We need to offer it to her. She would never ask. She's still so formal with us."

It bothered Beatrice. Unlike many immortals who chose not to grow attached to their mortal helpers, she considered most of their employees family. Granted, she was young. She knew it would be harder to bear the loss over hundreds, possibly thousands, of years. But Giovanni treated them the same, and he was far older than her.

Beatrice stripped, the feeling of cool air against her sensitive skin welcome after the stifling confinement of winter clothes. She now understood why her husband preferred to be naked. Any clothing was uncomfortable, though it was a discomfort she had learned to live with. She shuddered to think about the poor immortals who had lived through more restrictive fashion periods of history. Corsets? No, thank you.

But one had to blend. It kept the rest of the world comfortable. Beatrice still felt, in many ways, very human. Though there were differences between them, her best friend and assistant, Dez, was still her closest confidante. And though she'd once been a loner, she had created close relationships with her vampire family and her friends.

But Fina kept her distance. No doubt the revelations about Lorenzo had shaken her. But the woman was still here. She could have run away, but she'd stayed. Probably for the books.

Glancing at her husband, whose nose was back buried in his novel, she decided it was definitely for the books.

"You know what?" Beatrice mused. "She's kind of... you. A human female version of you."

"What?" He looked up, frowning. "Who's me?"

She smiled as she sauntered over to the bed. Dawn was still an hour or so away, so her mate would have plenty of energy. And Beatrice decided that he definitely needed distracting. She crawled up the bed and took the book from his hands, setting it on the side table.

"Mmm," he murmured. "Hello, my wife."

She straddled his legs and brushed the hair off his forehead. He'd been wearing his dark brown curls long again.

"Oh yeah," she said, leaning down to bite the edge of his ear. "You're definitely pulling off the sexy-yet-distracted-professor thing."

"I am not distracted anymore."

He put both hands on her hips, teasing the lace of her panties where they lay on her skin. Now that sensation she enjoyed.

"I was saying that Serafina is a female, human version of you, Professor."

"Hmm." His fangs fell, and he traced them lightly over the skin on her neck. "That's Dottore to you. And let us conference on this particular topic at another time, signorina. I don't find it pertinent to the matter at hand." His hand stroked down and cupped her under her panties.

"Oh, Dr. Vecchio," she whispered. "I'm not sure we should be having this conversation. It seems so unprofessional."

"It's highly unprofessional." Giovanni swiftly rolled them over so she was under him, and within seconds the delicate lace panties were scraps on the floor.

Then Beatrice's husband proceeded to ace every single sexy-professor fantasy she'd ever had. With honors.

"You're incredibly detail oriented," she panted hours later. "Yay for me."

His cheeks were flushed with the blood he'd taken from the inside of her thigh. "I pride myself on being thorough."

"Well done."

He grabbed her chin and covered her mouth in a hard kiss that slowly turned soft as he settled next to her in bed. She could feel the dawn coming in her blood. Giovanni still slept during the day, and on mornings when she'd taken his blood, she could sleep a little herself. Her own special version of afterglow.

"You know," he said, his eyes closing, "if you think Serafina is a female version of me, then all she really needs to be happy is her own version of you, *tesoro*."

Beatrice smiled and slid over to rest next to him, her body relaxed but her mind humming. Another version of herself?

Thinking of the letters she'd spotted peeking out of Fina's briefcase, an idea began to form.

It was Christmas in Italy. Perhaps Beatrice could work a little magic of her own.

⚜

"YOU WANT ENZO AND ME TO JOIN YOU IN ROME?" FINA looked between Giovanni and Beatrice with wide eyes. "For Christmas? I am very flattered to be asked, but—"

"Don't feel flattered, Fina, feel welcome," Beatrice urged her. "Please join us. We don't know many people in the city, and we'd love to have you and Enzo along. Surely you won't be working while he's on holiday from school."

"Well no, but—"

Giovanni said, "Holidays are always so much more enjoyable with children around."

"Even though you heathens don't exchange presents until January," Beatrice muttered.

He turned to her. "Again? We're having this argument again?"

"Epiphany. I have to wait until January to get presents. So unfair."

"Such an American," Giovanni said before he turned back to Fina. "My housekeeper in Rome is beside herself that we came without Ben, though he is hardly a child any longer. Angela would be delighted to have both of you come with us."

Could she? Most Christmases with Enzo were quiet affairs. She would build a small *ceppo* and fill it with lights and small gifts, always letting Enzo put the star on the top. She hung gold lights in the house and baked the *panettone* recipe her grandmother had taught her.

"Sweet bread for a sweet year, my Serafina."

Gifts had often been small when Enzo was young and she didn't have much money to spare, but the little presents always appeared like magic to his child's eyes. Christmas was quiet. Simple. She liked it that way.

"*Per favore, Mama!* Please, please, can we go to Rome? I want to hear the pipes and flutes, and there are all the trees. Please, Mama! I can tell all my friends—"

"Enzo, we do not boast of generosity," she whispered to her son. "Dr. Vecchio and—"

"*Beatrice* and *Giovanni*," her employer said, smiling, "would be very happy if you joined them." Then Giovanni nudged Enzo's shoulder and said, "And you should definitely hear the *zampognari* and *pifferai*. Though I warn you, some are quite bad." He laughed. "We'll find some good ones for you."

"Please, Fina," Beatrice said. "We're staying until the Epiphany, and we'd love it if you would join us." She paused. "And while I know you won't officially be working, there is a possibility that I'll be able to search the Vatican Library for more information regarding the mission letters. I'd love to have your help."

Fina tried to stop the color she could feel rising in her cheeks. "The Vatican Library?" Where Zeno Ferrara worked?

Surely Beatrice didn't intend...

"I wrote to my friend Zeno before we came," Beatrice said. "And I think he might have an idea who the priest in Rome was. I'm sure we'd be allowed to visit the library."

Giovanni frowned. "You wrote to Zeno?"

"Of course," Beatrice said. "Didn't I tell you?"

They exchanged a look that Fina couldn't interpret because her mind was racing.

Beatrice continued. "You two have exchanged letters, haven't you? About some of the collection here?"

"Yes," she said. "I... Yes, Signor Ferrara and I have corresponded. He's been very helpful."

"Excellent! I'm sure he'd enjoy meeting a colleague with so many of the same interests. Zeno is passionate about preservation."

There went her stomach. This was ridiculous. She was not a schoolgirl. "Passionate?"

"Oh yes," Giovanni said, smiling at his wife. "Zeno is a man of very strong passions. About books and... history. And terrorizing his assistants."

"Ignore him," Beatrice said. "Zeno's lovely. He worked in the Italian resistance during World War II, did you know that? When he was still a priest. I believe he's from Naples originally. I think he was quite the problem child within the church."

"That's fascinating."

Rome for Christmas? Taking Enzo to see the lights and music of the great city. Sharing lodging and meals—best not to think about that one—with her employers, who were quite obviously trying to make her a friend.

Seeing the Vatican Library.

Possibly meeting the man—the vampire—who'd been the subject of so many flights of imagination.

"A man of very strong passions," Giovanni had said.

Oh, Nonna, she thought. *You didn't teach me anything about this.*

What would her nonna say? A quiet family Christmas with her son or the mysteries of the Vatican Library and a holiday with vampires?

She knew exactly what Nonna would say.

"Pack your red underthings. Red is good luck."

"I'll go," Fina said, watching Enzo erupt with joy. "We'll go. Thank you for the invitation."

CHAPTER 2

Vatican City, Italy

Zeno Ferrara erupted from the table. "You are an idiot. A brainless, directionless idiot! Has the collar cut off all the circulation to your head?"

The young priest paled and stepped back. "But Brother Zeno—"

"And I am not your brother anymore!" He raked his hands through the hair that hung in his eyes. He needed a haircut. Again. But if these stupid young priests didn't stop misfiling his documents, he was never going to leave the archives.

The young human took another step back. "Are you going to bite me?" he whispered.

Zeno's head turned to the vaulted ceiling of his workroom. "Father God," he shouted, "save me from imbeciles before it comes to murder."

He heard the footsteps behind him and spun in a blur.

"Please stop scaring the young ones, Zeno." Arturo Leon raised a lazy eyebrow as he entered the room. "It's getting harder and harder to find you assistants."

That prompted a flurry of arguments in Latin between the two men. Old arguments they'd had for decades, with a few new digs thrown in. Zeno barely noticed when the young priest who'd lost the box of eighteenth-century correspondence slipped out of the room.

"I never thought I'd say this, my friend, but I believe you need a holiday." Arturo sat down at the table and crossed his legs, examining the odd assortment of papers, inks, quills, pens, magnifying loupes, and different artificial lights that decorated the center of the table. Zeno zipped around the rows of bookshelves, looking for the box he'd set out the night before. The box that had been misfiled somewhere within the cavernous room Zeno considered his own.

He finally stopped the blur of movement, appearing before the old priest with a grey document box in his hands. A box that looked exactly like the thousands of others that filled the room. A single string of numbers on the front was the only identifier.

"It may be in here." Zeno set it down on the table. "And I don't have time for a holiday."

"You do realize how odd that sounds coming from someone who is immortal."

"Yes, yes. But Vecchio and Beatrice will be here in an hour. And while three hours would have been more than enough time for me to go through the letters from California and find the ones they are looking for, now I cannot even find the box. Because of idiots with more devotion than brains!"

"Careful, Zeno. And why are we allowing Vecchio into the archives? He's a known thief."

"That all depends on how you define thief. He's a scholar. A respected one. His other skills are secondary, and it's not like you haven't used them in the past."

Arturo sniffed. "I don't know what you're talking about."

Zeno grinned. "Liar. Only one man could have procured

that very elusive—and inconvenient—gospel from Ethiopia. How many copies were there?"

"Only two."

"And now both are tucked away in your secret rooms, Arturo. And Vecchio is granted access to mine. I don't expect any objections."

"You presume much, Ferrara."

Zeno ignored Arturo, who'd been no more than a baby when Zeno had been turned in 1938. Now the child had become an old man, a powerful one. In charge of all immortal clergy and laypeople attached to the Catholic Church, Arturo wasn't a bad sort of human. In fact, Zeno considered him more of a friend than any others of the stuffy Church bureaucracy. The fact that he had to wade through their politics still chafed, even though he'd been doing it for over sixty years.

But he had more freedom and resources here than anywhere else, and the documents, the *letters*, were his calling.

They filled the cavernous room, missives from all over the world, stretching back as long as humans had taken pen to paper or parchment to communicate with others at a distance. He found the letters, procured any with even a passing link to the church, and then he dissected them. The authors, the recipients. Where and when were they written? Who did they mention? Correspondence was his passion.

The modern blasphemy of email, his bane.

Mostly Zeno was left alone, which suited him. He'd been released from his earthly vows ten years after he'd been made immortal as he'd felt unable to serve the church and remain steadfast in immortality. It was one thing for a human to reform at age thirty-five and take vows to God for the next forty years. Quite another to face an eternity of sacrifice with no end in sight. Zeno decided he could serve God far better if he retained his sanity. And his humor.

Maybe the young priests didn't see his humor, but it was there.

Sometimes.

The bits of socializing he did were with others of his kind. His life was his work. History was written by the victors, but the letters... Letters told the true tale. Zeno Ferrara specialized in the discovery of secrets hidden within the handwritten word.

He glanced at the letter from Beatrice De Novo, whom he'd met only two years before. He'd known her mate far longer and was enormously pleased that his old friend had found a wife who was so like-minded. Beatrice was a delight, though he'd never cease arguing with her about the sacrilege of electronic communication.

Thank God computers had no place in his library.

The letters. Again. His eyes stole back to them. Letters were truth. Not only the words written but how they were written. What pace did the pen keep upon the page? Where did the writer hesitate? Where did she rush? Sometimes he could fancy the pen in his own hand, the letters stretching out across his skin.

Giovanni and I will be in Rome over Christmas, and I'm really hoping you'll have some insight into this set of documents. If you have any of the complementary letters or know anything about the writer, we'd be so grateful, Zeno. We'll be in Perugia before we travel to Rome.

Perugia. Vecchio had an enormous private library in Citta di Castello, though Zeno had never visited. The librarian there...

Serafina Rossi.

He could see her name written neatly across the bottom of the very professional letters she'd written to Zeno about one matter or another. He always enjoyed answering them because the woman asked excellent questions, and after some correspondence, her letters contained a prim wit that intrigued him. The handwriting told him she was young and educated. But it told him nothing of her hair. Or her eyes.

Which were really none of his business, were they?

Except he wanted to know. More than one of his acquaintances had mentioned the "unique charms of the Vecchio Library," and he doubted they were talking about the bookcases or the stained glass.

What did she look like as she wrote to him? Did she have long hair, tied back as she worked? Was it short, mussed from hands tugging it in concentration? Did she wear glasses?

He had a weakness for women in glasses.

Did she curl over her desk as she wrote her very proper responses to him or sit upright with shoulders held carefully?

Did her lips purse when she wrote his name?

Her signature vexed him. The neatness of her given name was misleading. It was the sensual dip and swell when she signed *Rossi* that had caught Zeno's attention.

Fina.

Beatrice had once referred to the librarian as Fina in a letter.

Fina. Shortened form of Serafina, a name drawn from the Biblical "seraphim." Hebrew in origin. It meant "the burning ones."

A fiery name signed with such control.

Fina.

What would it look like in her own hand? Would the *F*'s angled upstroke be pointed like a dagger? Would the downstroke dip and swell beneath the line?

Zeno felt his lips curve into a smile. Over their two years of correspondence, he had to admit he'd developed a bit of a preoccupation with the woman. She understood passion for work as he did. He would be most intrigued to see Fina sign her first name.

Perhaps she would accompany Vecchio and Beatrice.

But probably not. Beatrice had mentioned a child who lived on the property, and it was doubtful that a young woman with a family would want to be away during the Christmas holiday. There were things to celebrate. Gifts to exchange.

Rubbing the silver-dotted stubble he'd let grow for months, Zeno tried to remember the last time he'd celebrated Christmas. The 1980s? Surely it hadn't been that long. But then he rarely took holidays. The few bits of leisure time he indulged in were spent with the two other immortals in Vatican City, playing the hardest, fastest football the three could manage without tearing up the carefully manicured lawns. Both the other vampires were priests and needed the physical challenge as much as he did. He really ought to take up mountain climbing again, but that would take too much time away from work.

Nobody understood the work.

He dove back into the box of letters, smiling when he found the one he'd been hunting.

Mission San Jose, 1798
    My dear Pietro, you cannot imagine this land we have found...

"YOU'RE HERE."

Giovanni looked up from his notebook to see his old friend, but the vampire was looking past him. He glanced over his shoulder to see Beatrice and Fina following him down the hall. He muffled the smile. It seemed that Beatrice had not been far off in her suspicions. Clever woman.

"Ferrara." Giovanni held out his hand, startling the man back to awareness. "So good to see you again. What has it been? Seven years or so?"

Zeno frowned. "What are you talking about? I received a letter from you in April."

"Of course." He held out a hand for Beatrice's. "I know you met my lovely wife last year."

"Zeno," Beatrice said. "So good to see you again. I cannot thank you enough for your help with this. Between the four of us, I just know we're going to track down this manuscript."

"The four of us," Zeno repeated.

Was Giovanni the only one who noticed the man's eyes darting to Fina repeatedly? He doubted it as the woman's face had taken on more than a bit of color.

"Yes," Beatrice said. "I know you've corresponded, but Zeno, let me introduce Fina to you. Serafina Rossi, our librarian in Perugia. Fina, this is Zeno Ferrara, former priest, handwriting expert, and terror of the Vatican."

"Hello." Zeno held out his hand and folded both of them around Fina's palm when they touched. "Ignore her. She married a fire vampire, so she's clearly not sane. It is such a pleasure to finally meet you, Signora Rossi."

"*Signorina* Rossi," Fina answered quietly. "Please, call me Fina. And it is a pleasure to meet you as well, Signor Ferrara." She looked around the room with a slight smile. "The scope of your work... You have understated it in your letters. It is monumental. Detailed handwriting and historical analysis on so many documents. I cannot imagine such a project. Truly a work for the ages."

"Please, you must call me Zeno." He couldn't keep his eyes off her. "I have been so impressed with the reports I have heard from Perugia. I understand the collection was completely unorganized when you arrived."

Beatrice couldn't stop the smile no matter how much she bit her lip.

The two librarians wandered toward the worktable, chattering like old friends, and Giovanni sidled up to his wife.

"Do you see it?" she asked almost silently, well aware of Zeno's sharp hearing. No matter, the vampire's gaze was locked on Fina's, rapt in every word that left her mouth.

"I see it."

"They're *perfect* for each other. I'd forgotten how handsome Zeno is. Nothing like you, but he definitely has the rumpled-professor-sexy going on."

"Is that supposed to be flattering?" He tried not to laugh at her. "It's certainly a face that drew much attention before he joined the church."

She gasped a little. "Zeno's a reformed scoundrel? Exactly what Fina needs! How did I miss this?"

"Perhaps because it is none of your business."

"Pfft." She punched him playfully in the stomach. "Whatever. I've got an eternity for whatever business needs doing. This is going to be great."

He stopped and put a hand on the small of her back. "She's human, *tesoro*."

"So was I."

Her eyes told him she knew exactly what he was saying.

"There are no guarantees of happily ever after here," Giovanni said.

She smiled a little ruefully. "That's life, isn't it? No guarantees about anything. We make the best of what we have. Every day. And I have a feeling those two have been putting off really *living* for too long."

How could he not kiss her?

"Meddler," he whispered as their lips parted.

"I know." She swiftly kissed the corner of his mouth. "Since I don't have any presents—"

"You're getting presents! You just get them in January."

"I have to amuse myself somehow."

"I'm glad you're amused."

"Gio, what would you have done if I hadn't wanted to turn?"

His smile fell. "Come. We should get started. I can hear the priests' nervous pacing at the thief among their books."

TWO HOURS LATER THEY HAD FOUND ALL THE LETTERS from the young priest in California that Zeno suspected he had in the collection. There might have been more, but there was no way of knowing. Between him and Beatrice, they'd checked every box of unexamined correspondence from the New World and found three more letters on top of the seven he'd found before. Combined with the letters from the Roman priest, they constituted a total of twenty-five documents.

They began sorting by date, the letters from Brother Rafael in California on one side, the ones from Brother Pietro in Rome on the other.

Zeno tried to focus on the letters and not the distracting Fina Rossi.

When she walked in, he'd known it was her. Zeno didn't know why or how, he just knew. It wasn't her thick hair the color of chestnuts or the deep brown eyes, for he hadn't known she possessed those. Or her set of sensuously full lips. Or her rather stunning figure.

Perhaps it was the look of quiet excitement on her face. Serafina of the intriguing letters would be quietly excited to visit the famed Vatican Library. Perhaps it was the very professional black briefcase she carried with a hint of whimsy in the red-striped lining that peeked from an open pocket.

Perhaps he simply knew. From her blood, the pulse of which heightened the moment their eyes met. From her scent, which was touched with vanilla and almonds as if the scent of crumbling paper perfumed her skin.

Zeno wanted to write his name across that skin. Trail the ink over the soft white of her arm and lose his stained fingers in the fall of her hair.

His reaction knocked him sideways. Zeno had not wanted a woman like that in a long, long time.

"What is this manuscript you mentioned, Beatrice?" He had to stop fantasizing about Fina's skin. This wasn't the time.

"*Mnrf.*" Beatrice took the pencil from her mouth. "I have a client looking for a manuscript detailing wine-cultivation practices in California during the mission period. He's eccentric. He told me that a priest working at one of the missions had written it, but he had no idea who the priest was or where this manuscript might have gone. I'd put it off for a while until I found a clue in another of the letters in my collection."

"The ones that Gio sent to Fina?" He raised his head and winked at the woman, only to see she'd put on reading glasses to look closer.

Her lips were pursed, her hair twisted up in a knot secured with a pencil.

Dear God...

She smiled. "I believe this was in another set of letters. Giovanni had already sent me the ones here because they were written by a Roman priest and he thought they belonged with the Vatican correspondence in the Vecchio Library in Perugia."

"I've heard what an impressive collection it is."

Her eyes lit as she talked about her work. It was... entrancing.

"It is so diverse," she said. "At first I could make nothing of the theme, but over time I began to see that all the documents—save for a few pieces here and there—related to the virtue and progress of humanity. It is a primer, so to speak, of the ideal classical individual. A map of self-improvement, if you will, gathered through the greatest periods of human achievement."

He saw Giovanni grimace and suspected some of the rumors he'd heard about the fire vampire's sire must be correct.

"A fascinating collection then. I hope to see it someday."

There was the rush of her blood again. He didn't think she feared him, so it must be pleasure? Excitement to share her work?

"Of course, Signor Ferrara—"

"Zeno."

"Zeno." Her pulse didn't slow. "We often have visiting scholars. You would be most welcome."

How many of those scholars came to examine the books and how many to see the beautiful, demure director of the Vecchio Library? How many were vampires like himself? He felt his fangs drop on instinct, so he looked back at the table, not wanting her to notice.

She had turned back to her own work by the time he wrestled his instincts under control.

He did not become possessive of humans. It was not his priority, and he had chosen not to indulge that aspect of his immortal nature. His assignations with women over the years had been friendly but casual. Respectful, always. For the offer of blood, the giving of it, was as sacred to him now as it had ever been. In war. In the sacrament. Blood was life.

But Zeno would be the worst sort of liar if he didn't confess that he wanted Fina's.

Though young vampires such as him could be highly

possessive, he'd always fought against it. He had given up all possessions when he joined the church. Given up the wealth gained through lying and manipulation. And though he drew a generous salary for his work at the Vatican, he lived simply.

He had learned as a human: Earthly possessions had a way of owning their master.

And to possess one such as her? Infinitely more dangerous.

"I think I have something," she said, flipping the paper over. "It is in the postscripts on the back. I had overlooked them because they don't refer to anything related to wine. But if we're looking for the identity of the writer, I think they might be compelling. I believe these two priests were quite close, as it appears the Roman priest—"

"Brother Pietro."

"Yes, Pietro—might have been counseling Rafael in some spiritual matter."

Zeno said, "I've just sorted these and I'm beginning to skim the contents. I believe you're correct. Look at 1801."

Zeno and Fina moved down the table, standing across from each other as they looked for the correct letter and its response.

"Here," she said. "In May. This is what I saw. In the second to last paragraph, it reads: 'I urge you, brother, to fight against this temptation. For you know there can be no end that will satisfy God or yourself. Pray for guidance and confess to your brothers there. But do not... do not be tempted.' Please forgive my Spanish; it is not the best." She stopped and looked at Zeno. "What was in the letter before this one? To what is he referring?"

Zeno found the one dated before the letter Fina had read. He skimmed it, but there was nothing. Nothing but the day-to-day life of the mission. Concern about a sudden disease that had struck the animals. He flipped it over to examine the back of the letter. Eight small words sat lonely on the back of the page.

I cannot stop my thoughts turning to Antonia.

"Antonia," he said. "He cannot stop thinking of *Antonia*. Had Father Rafael been in love?"

Beatrice moved next to him, taking the letter from his hands. "Who was she?"

Giovanni asked, "Is there any way of knowing? She could have been anyone."

Fina said, "She was obviously known to both of them. A relative of Pietro's perhaps?"

Beatrice asked, "What kind of records does the church keep on eighteenth-century Franciscans? Anything?"

"Hmm." Zeno thought he might know of someone who would know, but the human would be sleeping at two in the morning. "Let me work on that tomorrow. For now, let's see what else we can find."

Beatrice frowned. "Not that I don't love a good mystery, but does this have anything to do with a manuscript on early viticulture?"

"You want to know where your book went, no?" Zeno growled. "It seems to me that the more we find out about Brother Rafael, the more we might be able to trace his manuscript. Fina, do you have the next?"

"The next after the mention of Antonia is the one I read before," she said. "It would be Rafael's turn to respond."

He looked up; her heart was racing again.

"Are you all right, *cara?*"

"Fine." She flushed. "Thank you."

"Are you tired? I forget that you are not a monster of the night like me."

That got a smile out of her. "I'd hardly call you monstrous."

"Wait till you see me in a temper."

A crooked smile curved her lips. "I cannot imagine."

Giovanni burst into laughter, and Zeno threw a sharpened pencil at his face, which he caught easily.

"The next letter, Zeno. Before I tell her all your secrets."

"Very well." He walked down the line. "Ah, here. 'My dear brother, only you know how much I honor her. Only you know how pure our love. How can such be called a sin? For I carry her in my heart in this foreign place. She is light.'" He glanced up, feeling Fina's eyes on him. "'Though I know she cannot be mine, still I long for her happiness.'"

Wordlessly, Fina picked up the next letter and scanned it.

"Here, just at the bottom: 'Though your sincerity is honorable, yet our faith must bid you to abandon this, brother. For other purposes mark your steps. Purposes far greater than earthly temptations.'"

Zeno found the next letter.

"'Do the scriptures not write that God himself is love? Brother, I cannot abandon hope when I have no word that hope is lost. For the lady's devotion remains true, though I am oceans away from her. I go to Santa Maria tomorrow. I must pray.'"

Fina read again, already finding the next letter Father Pietro had written.

"'My dear brother, surely you must see that there is no hope. For our vows are eternal—'"

Zeno broke in. "Obviously that's not true."

Fina smiled and continued, "'—and our work is God's own. What comparison is there between... fleshly gratification and heavenly delight?'"

Zeno cocked his head. "I'm rather sure there can be both. Very well, here's the next from our boy, Rafael. Don't buy it, brother," he muttered to the page. "'He writes, 'And yet, my dear Pietro, my devotion is steadfast. Had all hope been lost for me, I know you would have written of it. Therefore, I shall hope. And though an ocean separate us, and the world condemn us, I believe heaven does not.'"

Beatrice crossed to read over Zeno's shoulder. "That's beautiful."

Fina read, "'I cannot deceive you that the lady remains unattached, though faithful to her family and to God. Her position in society is uncertain should she remain unwed. And what have you, a poor Franciscan, to offer her, even were you to abandon your vows? I plead with you to flee from this strange attachment.'"

"A harsh fate," Giovanni said. "Even if Rafael had abandoned his vows, he stood to return to his lady with nothing. Would he even be able to return to Spain? Was Antonia Spanish or Italian? It seems clear that though Rafael was of the Spanish church, Pietro was a Roman."

Beatrice picked up the next letter and handed it to Zeno.

"Only one line at the bottom of the page: 'My soul is in agony. Surely God must save me from this.'"

"'Pray, my brother,'" Fina read back to him, her voice aching. "'For God does not desire his children to suffer pain such as this. Pray and devote yourself to your work.'"

"'I cannot pray,'" Zeno read from the next, his own heart beating once as he listened to her. "'For what are empty words against this despair? Without her, the light is gone. My work brings me no joy without the contemplation of her countenance. I see her smile within the sun. Her hair in the trailing vines I tend. I can only touch them since I cannot reach her.'"

"'I beg of you, brother'"—there were tears at the corners of Fina's eyes—"'to tend your vines as you would tend the one you love. What purpose is there in this world without the Lord's mission? I mourn for your pain. Devote yourself to God's work as you would devote yourself to her. For in this you must find the satisfaction lost to you in this life. And know that this world is only a prelude to the next. There is still hope.'"

Was there still hope?

Zeno skimmed through the last letter. He read it. Read it again, the words locked in his mind. Then he let his eyes meet Fina's as he recited Rafael's last missive. "'I will come for her. I have no choice. She is all that is light and beauty in my life. My soul is but a mirror of her own. My heart, her twin in devotion. Surely God cannot condemn us. Surely the world must be kind. I will come for her, though oceans separate us. I have a plan. Tell my love to wait for me. I beg you, my brother, tell her I shall come. For what is an ocean against eternity?'"

Zeno let his eyes fall back to the page. "Presidio de Monterey, 1803."

CHAPTER 3

Rome, Italy

F*or what is an ocean against eternity?*
He was so much more than she had imagined. Fina lay in her bed, breathless at the memory of Zeno's voice, reading the letters as if the two of them had *been* the lovers, parted by fate.

The dark tangle of his hair, touched with silver at the temples. The laugh lines at the corners of his eyes. He must have been in his forties when he'd been turned. Unusual, from what she had learned. But then what did she know? She was a child in his world, stumbling through life with her organizer and briefcase, assisting those far wiser than herself.

He seemed so very human... until he did not. She could see the flashes of predatory awareness in him when his temper slipped. The body that moved just a little too fast. She did suspect that he could be the "terror of the Vatican" as Beatrice had called him. For surely a man—a vampire—like Zeno was no tame thing.

How did he feel so familiar? Was it his letters, which had so perfectly captured his mercurial personality and gruff humor? It had to be. Fina had felt immediately comfortable despite having never met him before. This stranger. This vampire! It was as if their minds were already familiar even if their bodies were not.

The way he'd watched her... Even miles away from Vatican City, in the luxurious Vecchio home, she could still feel his eyes.

"Mama?"

She heard Enzo's sleepy voice from the hall. They'd only returned an hour before dawn. Fina was both exhausted and wired by the night. She lay in her bed, dressed for sleep, but sleep did not find her.

"Come in, Enzo."

Her boy pushed open the door. Twelve years old. Where had the years gone? Soon he would be a man. Her heart ached a little at the knowledge even as she felt a surge of pride. She had done this. No one had helped her, save for Giovanni's son. She had raised Enzo. Loved him. Taught him. And she had done well.

Enzo rolled onto the side of the bed, rubbing sleepy eyes. "Did you just get home? How was the library?"

"It was fascinating, darling, but why are you awake?"

"I heard you come in, I think. The gate..."

"Ah, of course." The gate to the massive old house was very close to his room. "I'll be sure to be quieter tonight. We were talking loudly, I think."

He nodded, his eyes falling closed. "I should go back to bed."

"Yes, do. I'll be sleeping late today. Do you have plans?"

"Angela said something about the market." He yawned and sat up. "And Rudy and I are helping her decorate the house. She's fun."

"Such a good boy." She ruffled his hair. "What would I do without you?"

"Get lots of work done and be very boring."

"Oh." She groaned and rolled into the pillow as he laughed. "You know your mama."

"Did you have fun?" he asked. "You sounded like you had fun at the library."

"I did," she said. "It's a wonderful thing to love your work."

"Good." He leaned down and kissed her cheek. "Good night. Good day, I mean." He bared his teeth. "Soon you'll be just like the vampires."

She laughed, but within minutes of Enzo closing the door, Fina had fallen asleep.

When she woke, it was to the dip of her bed. Fina opened her eyes to see Beatrice leaning over, fangs hanging down in her smiling mouth.

"Aah!" Fina sat bolt upright, scrambling toward the headboard.

"Hey!" Beatrice said. "Sorry I surprised you, but you will not believe what I found out today!"

"Are you going to bite me?"

Finally understanding that Fina was terrified, Beatrice leaned back. "What? No."

"But your—" Fina motioned to her mouth, heart pounding. "They're just... long and—and sharp. And you're not going to bite me?"

Beatrice cocked her head. "Do you want me to bite you?"

"No!"

"This"—she waved at her mouth—"happens for a lot of reasons. Excitement is one of them. Sorry, I was just so jazzed about what I found. I'll have to keep that in mind." She smiled, and Fina noticed her fangs were a little shorter. "Sorry."

"It's okay." It really wasn't, but Fina did understand her employers were not human. She knew that. Maybe she just didn't know that as well as she'd thought.

Fangs. Long, sharp fangs.

Zeno would have them too.

"You were the last one sleeping," Beatrice said.

"Oh." She looked toward the window. The sun was already down, and she could hear a football skittering around the cobblestones of the courtyard below. "Enzo?"

"Mm-hmm."

There were other voices too. Male voices. Shouting something.

"Mitto!"

The skidding ball.

"Mittere!"

Another kick.

"Misi."

"Missus!"

Fina frowned. "Is that...?"

"Gio invited Zeno over for Angela's dinner. I think he's going to the market with us later too."

She sat up, totally forgetting that Beatrice's fangs had scared her. "Zeno's here? And they're—"

"Declining Latin verbs while they kick around a soccer ball? Yes. Yes, they are. My husband thinks Latin is God's language and everyone should know it."

Fina started laughing just as they started on *habeo.*

"My son, your husband, and Zeno are... They're being such... There is an English word, but I cannot remember."

"Nerds," Beatrice said, joining in the laughter. "They are being really, really big nerds right now."

"Yes." She couldn't stop laughing. "Yes, that is the word."

Beatrice stood and walked to the window where the kicking and shouting had ceased.

She waved at whomever she saw and said, "I think Zeno heard you laughing. He's got that hungry, dazed expression on his face."

And all of a sudden, she was thinking about fangs again. "Hungry?"

"Not the kind of hungry you're thinking."

She flushed and Beatrice laughed.

"Okay, *now* it's the kind of hungry you're thinking. Oh my, I bet he loves that blush you have."

"It's incredibly embarrassing. I've blushed since I was a girl. I hate it."

"You better get used to the fangs, Fina, because when this goes up"—she pointed the finger of her right hand straight —"these go down." The other hand came up, two fingers dropping like fangs.

"Oh." Well, that was more than she'd ever expected to know about vampire sex. "That's... interesting."

"Yes, it is." Beatrice grinned. "You and Zeno couldn't keep your eyes off each other last night. I noticed."

"Was I that obvious?" She paused, thought about what Beatrice had said. "It was more than just me?"

"Oh yeah. What kind of letters have you two been writing for the past couple of years?" She waved out the window again, then pointed down and nodded. "Gio wants me to come down and meet them. I'll hold Zeno off from charging up the stairs until you're ready."

"Please do."

Why was she talking about this with her employer? But employers didn't break into your room and jump on your bed, excited about a discovery. They didn't call their husband a nerd while that husband was playing football with your son. They didn't tease you about a man—vampire—you were dangerously attracted to.

"Beatrice?"

She paused at the door. "Yeah?"

"Are we friends now?"

Beatrice smiled. "I'm trying to be. I don't do very well with the whole scary-vampire-lording-over-humans thing yet. Give me a few hundred years or so, and I'm sure I'll have it down."

Fina smiled. "I don't have many friends. I didn't want to assume."

"Assume away." She glanced down the hall. "But don't take long to get ready. Those boys are champing at the bit."

Fina didn't know exactly what that meant, but she quickly dressed and hurried downstairs.

And she did it wearing red lace under her clothes.

Well, Nonna, life certainly is interesting now.

⁂

BEATRICE WATCHED ZENO AS FINA CAME DOWN THE STAIRS. The hungry look was back, but his cheeks had color, so she knew he'd fed recently. Smart of him. He must have sensed Fina was cautious about vampires, so he was being considerate and not taxing his self-control. Zeno was still talking with Enzo, debating soccer, which they both avidly followed. They shared a love for the same Italian club, and conversation seemed to swing between perfect excitement and utter despair. Often within the same sentence. When Fina came down, she joined them and the three talked like old friends while Beatrice watched from across the room.

Excellent. Things were progressing nicely.

Gio bent down and kissed her temple. "Happy, darling?"

"I'd be happier with presents." It was just so fun to annoy him about the present thing.

"You're hopeless."

"No, I'm present-less."

"You poor deprived girl."

"Have you ever thought about trying to steal Zeno away from the Vatican?"

He narrowed his eyes at the change in subject. "Many times. He's a quiet sort, but I know for a fact he can take care of himself. Doesn't attract much attention, and he's a bulldog when it comes to research. He'd be an ideal employee. Previously, I'd not had anything to tempt him away from his comfortable cave in Rome, but now..."

She looked up at him innocently. "Look how helpful I'm being, meddling like this. You're so lucky to have me."

Giovanni smiled, his green eyes sparkling. "I know exactly how lucky I am. And I have to say I approve. As long as Fina continues to like him, of course. I have no interest in replacing her, but I think she could use some help."

"He'd be perfect for it. And I'd breathe easier knowing that there was someone we trusted at the library. Someone stronger than a human."

"I've been thinking along the same lines." The humor fled Giovanni's face as he sat down next to her. "My reputation and Emil's protection have so far warned off anyone who might cause trouble, but as word of Andros's books spreads, I don't want to take chances. My sire's collection contains secrets I'm not even aware of. There could be others threatened by it. Even someone as well trained as Rudy would not be enough."

"So, Zeno or no Zeno, we need to find a vampire to live and work in Perugia."

"I think so."

She looked back at the pair, who were totally engaged. "Well," she said, "hopefully this will end well for everyone."

"Let's get business out of the way, then go find some Christmas pipers for Enzo, eh?"

"Sounds good." She raised her voice a little. "Hey, let's go over what we found today, and then we'll eat."

All business, Zeno and Fina walked over to the dining room while Enzo drifted to the kitchen, uninterested in the "library stuff."

The excitement made Beatrice's blood run. She'd been on and off the phone all day with Dez in California and the priest whom Zeno had referred her to last night. What they'd put together brought Rafael's manuscript much closer than she ever would have expected.

"After we looked over the letters last night, I had my assistant in California look up some of the ship manifests and passenger lists we've collected from that period."

"Why did you collect those?" Fina asked. "Just curious."

"To examine what was being shipped in and out of California at the time. Most of our interest has actually been in the cargo, but I had Dez look for any passengers out of Monterey from 1803. We know that was the last letter that Rafael sent. Know that he told his friend he had a plan. So I started looking there."

"Meanwhile," Zeno said, "I asked a certain priest who specializes in genealogy to look into Father Pietro. There were only so many Franciscans named Pietro who came from prominent families in Rome during that time. And from his handwriting and vocabulary, he had more than a church education. Pietro came from wealth."

They all sat comfortably at the dining table, Giovanni and Beatrice on one side, Zeno and Fina on the other. Beatrice had to bite back a smile at how close the two were sitting to each other.

Zeno continued, "There was one Franciscan who stood out. The third son of a very prominent family, his brothers had taken over the estate, but he was educated for the church. Why he became a Franciscan, I do not know. But there were records of his family because they owned quite a lot of land and were minor nobility." Then he smiled. "And what we found is very interesting."

"A sister?" Fina asked. "Was there a sister?"

Zeno's eyes locked with hers. "How did you know?"

"I didn't. Just suspected. How else would Rafael have been so confident that Pietro could give Antonia his message? She had to have been part of his family. A sister seemed the most likely."

"Very clever," Zeno said. "Yes, Pietro had a sister named Antonia. There was a mention of her marrying in 1805, but after that, we could find nothing. And nothing about the identity of whom she married either."

"So we don't know if they found their way back to each other?" Fina looked stricken.

"Not necessarily," Beatrice said. "Dez found him. There were numerous Rafaels who sailed from California in 1803 and 1804, but only one with a name that jumped out at me. Rafael Szarka left the Presidio of Monterey in March of 1804. He sailed down to Mexico—well, Baja California—then back to Spain. After that, we have no idea."

"Szarka is not a Spanish name," Zeno said.

"No, it's Hungarian." Beatrice waved a hand. "Don't ask. I can't tell you. But this is our Rafael, I'm certain of it."

"So we know his name," Fina said. "And presumably he went back to Spain. But we have no idea what happened after that."

Zeno squeezed her hand where it lay on the table. "We'll keep looking, *cara*. This much progress is already far more than I would expect to learn in such a short time."

Giovanni nodded. "Now, let's eat. Then we will go show Enzo the city at Christmastime." He put his arm around Beatrice. "I think we're all ready for a little fun."

FINA COULDN'T REMEMBER THE LAST TIME SHE'D HAD SO much fun. Giovanni and Beatrice dragged them all over Rome. They gaped at churches and piazzas decorated with thousands of lights. They visited the giant Christmas tree near the Colosseum. They wandered past the shops near the Spanish Steps and took in the toys and luxury fashions that decorated the store windows.

Spending time with Zeno was effortless. The more she knew him, the more she liked, though she still hadn't caught a glimpse of the rumored fangs. He joked with Enzo, listening to everything the boy said, and appeared to truly enjoy their conversations, unlike some adults who only condescended to children. He took her arm with old-fashioned manners... but then, he *was* old-fashioned. He casually mentioned how Rome had changed over decades, but he still seemed to enjoy the modern lights and markets.

He was... perfect.

And he was a vampire. He would never die. Never grow older. She tried not to think too far ahead, but the simmering interest she'd nurtured over years of correspondence had heated to a full, rolling boil. She wanted him. And she suspected he wanted her. But was it only a casual interest in a woman or something more serious?

Fina didn't have casual affairs. In fact, Zeno spending time with Enzo broke one of her cardinal rules. The few men she'd dated over the years had never met her son. No relationship had become serious enough for that. But Enzo had already met the vampire, and she could see the hero worship starting to take hold. The boy had no paternal figures in his life—her own papa and brothers no longer acknowledged her—and she knew her son was hungry for male interaction, especially as he'd grown older. It was part of the reason he looked forward to Giovanni's visits.

"Fina." Zeno called her over to one stall as they strolled through the market of the Piazza Navona. "Look at these!"

He was laughing, holding up gaudy earrings with flashing Christmas lights on them, only to have them short out when he held them up to his ears. He grinned and pulled a few euros out of his pocket to give to the vendor.

"No," she protested. "Look. They're..." She started to laugh. "Well, they're awful, aren't they? And they don't even work, Zeno."

He leaned down and took her arm, whispering in her ear, "They probably did, *cara*. But vampires and electronics do not get along well, do they?"

"Oh?" Then she remembered. Beatrice had told her the current all immortals carried in their touch, called *amnis*, wreaked havoc on anything electronic. She wasn't sure why. She smiled up at Zeno. "And here I thought you were only a Luddite."

"Oh, I am. Computers are not my friend." He hadn't leaned away from her ear. "I prefer a hands-on approach when I want to research something."

Her heartbeat took off. He was so close. Just beside her neck, his breath tickling above her scarf. The perfect position to kiss her. Or bite her. She looked around for Enzo, but he was in a circle surrounding a couple of street musicians with Beatrice and Giovanni.

"*Cara mia*...," Zeno said gruffly. "Surely you know."

She could hardly breathe. "Yes."

"And would you?"

"It... depends."

He pulled a little away to look into her eyes, but his arm was still linked with her own. "On what does it depend?"

Were those fangs behind his lips? He was murmuring, but was it because he did not want her to see him?

"It's not that you're what you are, Zeno. Maybe a little, but it is more that..." She glanced over at Enzo again. "I do not bring people into my son's life who are casual. I rarely date, and when I do—"

"Why would I be interested in *dating* you?"

Her heart plunged. Was that derision in his voice? How could she have been so wrong? Her face felt as if it were on fire.

"Dating," he continued, even as she looked for escape, "is a ridiculous modern concept. Why would I take you to the theater or the cinema once a week for months when I could work with you for one day and know you better? And I don't eat regular meals, not the kind you do. So dining is not an option. Dating is useless."

"But I—"

"We already suit each other, Fina. It was obvious before we even met."

Was she starting to see the side of him that was the "terror of the Vatican?" She could see his temper brewing.

"Zeno, I think we misunderstand each other."

"I am not interested in something casual. Do I look like a casual person?" His head swung around the marketplace. "I am older than everyone here, save Vecchio and that old vampire sitting by the fountain."

"There's a vampire by the fountain?" Her wide eyes looked over his shoulder.

"He's not dangerous—pay attention."

Her own temper piqued, she pulled her arm away and said, "I am not one of your assistants to order around, Zeno Ferrara. I may be a quiet person, but quiet does not equal meek."

"Are you afraid of me?" He stepped closer. "Is that what this is about?"

"No!"

"Then why do you step away from me?"

"I do not." Did she?

A pair of young men came up to them, clearly interested in the scene. She knew their type. Calling at the girls. Hungry to feed their ego with feminine embarrassment.

"Signorina, does he bother you?" one asked.

The other said, "Old brute, you should leave the lady alone." Then he laughed. "She is too pretty for you anyway. Signorina, run away with us! Leave the rude one. We know how to take care of a lady."

"Perhaps *both* of us can try," the other said, leering.

With a swiftness that was more than a little inhuman, Zeno turned to them. She could see the edge of his fangs when he gritted his teeth. He gripped both of them on the side of their necks and hissed, "Leave the piazza now, and do not ever speak to her again."

Without another word, both boys turned and left the square. They did not look at her. They did not turn back. There were no obnoxious comments thrown over their shoulders. It had all happened so quickly; no one in the crowd even turned to stare.

Speechless, she felt Zeno grab her hand. He pulled her to a secluded corner near the fountain, and she could see a cold-eyed man turn to watch them with narrowed eyes.

"Is that the vampire?" she whispered.

"Fina," he growled, raking his hand through his hair. "I am sorry. I have a possessive streak and—"

"Are we safe?"

"I would *never* hurt you."

"No, from that vampire over there."

He turned and hissed something in an unknown language.

Slavic, perhaps? With a grim smile, the other immortal melted into the night.

"I'm sorry," he said again. "I promise—"

"Would you ever use your... whatever that was on me?" Her eyes felt huge, blinking as if to clear the frightening image from her mind. "Like you did on those boys?"

"Fina, no." He leaned his forehead against her temple and she felt it in her hand, like a trickling of warm water stealing up her arm. "Do you feel that, *cara*?" he whispered.

"Yes."

"That is *amnis*."

"What you used on the boys."

"I can manipulate the human mind with it. I can move the earth with it. I feed it with mortal blood, and it keeps me alive, even after one hundred years on this earth."

She couldn't stop the shiver that overtook her. Zeno wrapped his arms around her shoulders and she felt it again, heating her skin. That warm trickle of energy spread over her limbs, as if an invisible blanket fell.

"I can use it to warm you. I can bring you extreme pleasure. But I will never use it to manipulate your will, Serafina. I promise you."

"How can I be certain?"

"Because I wish to use far more enjoyable methods of persuasion to convince you to accept me."

She looked up. "Accept you how?"

His dark brown eyes burned into hers. "As a lover. A friend. A part of your life. Your son's life."

"You do not wish to date me," she said breathlessly.

"We are beyond that. We know each other. Maybe not our bodies, because we have only just met. But my mind recognized yours. From the first letters. I have kept them all. Every one."

"I suspect you keep all your letters. Neatly filed. Organized by date and cross-referenced by mutual acquaintance."

A smile broke through his severe expression. "See? You do know me. But yours are the only ones I pull out to read over and over. Trying to guess who you are from the angle of your signature. They stay in my desk."

"I keep yours in my briefcase," she murmured.

"In the red-striped pocket?"

Her eyes went wide again. "How did you know?"

"Because I know you too." He bent down, lips brushing over her forehead. "The girl with the fiery name and the careful signature. Cautious Fina."

Her heart was going to beat out of her chest.

"Loyal Fina," he whispered as his nose touched hers. "Beautiful Fina."

His lips pressed against her own and she leaned into him, opening her mouth as Zeno's hands came to cup the back of her head. Soft, searching kisses turned into deep tangles of tongue and lips and teeth. She felt them, growing long in his mouth, the fangs that had so frightened her.

She pressed closer, devouring him. Swallowing the groan that came from her throat. He tasted of heat and wine. The tip of her curious tongue reached up to caress the length of one fang, and Zeno growled into her mouth. His hands fisted in her hair.

"Stop," he said against her lips. "We must stop now or I will steal you away. Then Giovanni would burn me alive for kidnapping his best employee."

A strangled laugh from her mouth. "Oh yes. I'm sure."

"No, really. Burning is what he does to his enemies." His thumb brushed the edge of her mouth, and when he pulled it away, she could see the smear of red. Had she cut her lip on his fangs? She hadn't felt a thing.

"The kissing." He closed full lips over the drop of her

blood, then teased her with a glimpse of his tongue running over one fang. "Mmm. The kissing comes with practice."

"Oh." And there was her face. On fire again.

Zeno smiled wickedly. "You're beautiful, Fina. And your taste..." His eyes flicked over her body. "I can't wait for practice."

"Zeno—"

"When does Enzo go to sleep?"

"What? I... I don't—"

"I can be patient, but I don't want to be." He took a step back. "Do you need patience?"

Did she?

No.

She wanted him to heat her blood again. To make her feel alive in ways she hadn't since she'd become a mother. She wanted Zeno to see the red lace under her clothes. She wanted to know just what he meant by practice.

"He'll go to sleep as soon as we get home," she said. "It's very late."

"Good."

He grabbed her hand and pulled her back to the market stalls in the piazza, carols playing on pipes and flutes filling the air while they walked under twinkling gold lights. When they got back to Giovanni and Beatrice, she could see her son rubbing his eyes. Fina realized it was almost midnight.

"Time to go, I think," she said cheerfully. "Enzo, did you have fun?"

She saw her son eying Zeno's hand as he held hers. The vampire showed no sign of letting her go anytime soon. Nor did she want him to. Still, the public declaration made her a little nervous.

Enzo looked from his mother's flushed face to Zeno, then back again. He smiled. "Yes. Very fun. But Gio was right. Some of those pipers were just terrible."

CHAPTER 4

Zeno sat back, leaning against the stone walls that lined the courtyard, closing his eyes as he listened to the comforting sounds of a family retiring for the night. He heard Angela's quiet snores in the downstairs bedroom. The guard's unobtrusive footsteps. Enzo's sleepy murmurs from the second story. Beatrice whispering something just past Zeno's hearing as she and Fina talked in the hall.

Giovanni came to stand beside him, holding out a glass of red wine. "You don't take spirits, am I correct?"

He shook his head. "Too strong. Wine is all I can handle."

Zeno was still young for an immortal, with keen senses that had not been dulled by centuries. While older vampires like Giovanni could enjoy the brandy or whisky he'd consumed as a human, Zeno's taste was still too sensitive. The heavy red wine, with its hints of earth and smoke and mushroom, was as complex as he could stand.

"Mmm," he said after the first sip. "My thanks. This is excellent."

"Do you need to speak to me?"

He curled one corner of his mouth up in a rueful smile. "Do I?"

Giovanni sat on the bench across from him. "She is under my aegis, Ferrara."

"Ah, I forget how old-fashioned you are."

"Not old-fashioned. Cautious."

Zeno shrugged. "You know I am a bastard. I have no sire and no political allegiance."

"You live in Rome but work within the church. I will admit that Emil Conti may not have required a formal pledge from you—"

"He has not."

"But that does not mean he has overlooked you. You could be an asset to him. He's aware of it."

"Conti's not a bad sort." He took another sip of wine. "But I have no interest in politics and power plays. I never have."

Giovanni finally smiled. "Why do you think I like you so much?"

"I desire her, Giovanni." All amusement fled his expression. "More than desire."

"If she is willing, I have no objection to a liaison of course. If your interest lies further—"

"I think it does."

Giovanni raised a skeptical eyebrow. "Think?"

"It does, dammit." He frowned and raked a hand through his hair. He really did need that haircut.

"Zeno—"

"I lost my temper in the market like a newly turned child," he said. "I thought of her when I had only her letters to hold. And now that I have met her in the flesh..."

"She's a lovely woman."

A bitter laugh escaped him. "For the first time in one hundred twenty years, there is something I want to possess.

And I haven't even slept with the woman yet. You know how this instinct will be once I have her."

Giovanni opened his mouth, then closed it. He thought for a moment before he spoke. "I do not know her well. I suspect you know more of her, though you've only just met in person. But I will say this: She is human. Do not waste time. The years stretch out before us, centuries with which to pace ourselves. She does not have that. She's young. But every second is precious."

"Do you object to our relationship?"

"Not at all."

"Thank you."

"I'm not her father, only her employer. And her necessary protector in our world." Giovanni smiled slowly. "Unless she has another, of course. You know the offer still stands."

"I cannot abandon my work."

"So don't." He sipped his whisky. "Take your precious letters with you. Or borrow them in batches to work on in Perugia. I'm sure you can persuade or bully Arturo into it. God knows you've scared away all the suitable assistants in Rome. There is more than enough room for both of you to work in the library there. She's alone, Zeno. Think about it. I need to hire someone to watch over her and the library. Wouldn't you like it to be you and not someone else?"

Zeno paused, knowing that to take Giovanni's offer would change the balance of his eternity. "I'll think about it."

He saw a light go on in Fina's bedroom on the third floor.

Giovanni stood and said, "Don't waste a minute."

Zeno set the unfinished glass of wine on the stone bench and walked into the house, up the three flights of stairs that led to her room, quietly conscious of the sleeping humans around him. They would not hear him. And he heard no sign of Giovanni and Beatrice. They had fled the property, affording Zeno and Fina privacy.

He tapped softly on the door, and she opened it. Her cheeks were delightfully flushed with the redness that so often marked them. She probably hated it, but it delighted him. Her lips looked like she'd been worrying them between her teeth.

"Invite me in," he whispered, tamping down his hunger.

She frowned. "Do I need to do that?"

"Yes." The innocent question made him grin. "But not for any supernatural reasons."

"Oh." She opened the door wider. "Please. Come in, Zeno."

He walked through the door and quickly turned, setting the lock for privacy. He held his finger to his lips as he walked toward her.

"Quiet," he whispered. Finally reaching her, he leaned down and brushed a kiss across her lips. "We must be quiet."

She clutched at the lapels of his coat, but he tugged it off. Then his shirt. He toed off his shoes. And while he did that, she started to undo the buttons on her blouse. He put a hand up to stop her.

"Why?" she said.

"I like to unwrap my own presents."

She smiled and let him slip the buttons loose to reveal dark red lace that barely covered her. It was the color of wine. Of blood. He grew even harder than he'd been, and his fangs fell in his mouth.

"Fina," he groaned as his mouth tasted the lace.

"Red for luck," she said.

"My luck or yours?"

"Both, I think."

He fought his instincts to take, take, *take* as he slipped the lace aside to taste her skin. Though he knew how to make his bite pleasurable, he did not want to try it their first time together. It might be too shocking, and he had plans to ensnare his little human quite thoroughly into his world.

"*Cara mia*," he whispered, pushing her back toward the bed. "We must be quiet, but I do not want to be."

"This time," she said, quieting him with her lips.

This time.

He smiled into her kiss, the possessive instincts assuaged. There would be a next time. And a next. In fact, Fina might not know it, but Zeno decided in that moment he had no intention of letting her go.

She laid herself before him, baring her body in the moonlight, and Zeno realized it was an entirely different kind of possession when the object of your desire offered herself. He had given up every worldly object in order that those *things* might not own him. But he surrendered himself to her arms, happy to claim Fina as his own.

"Mine," he whispered as he kissed down her body. The words didn't feel grasping or controlling. They were sweet on his tongue.

Because, in fact, she was the one who possessed.

He tasted her skin. The sweet arousal between her thighs. Fina's fingers clenched in his hair as she gasped with pleasure, and he decided perhaps he didn't need a haircut after all, because the quick pleasure-pain made him focus.

Focus.

She was soft. Mortal. He had to be careful. He heard her heart pounding. Could feel the rush of her blood.

When he finally entered her, he could not hide the fangs that grew long in his mouth, not even when he tried. He turned his head to the side but felt her hand pressing his cheek, forcing his gaze back to her. Forcing his lips to meet hers in a searing kiss.

"Fina."

"I do not fear you, Zeno."

He thrust harder, for every part of her accepted him in that moment. Fina stroked his fangs, cutting her tongue on the edge of them. Zeno took it. He only had so much control, after all. He sucked her tongue in his mouth, tasting the sweet tang of her blood. Like a drop of the finest wine, it slid down his throat.

Seconds later, she came again. A few moments after that, Zeno followed her.

And it was a lovely fall.

⟐

GIOVANNI HELD BEATRICE'S HAND AS THEY WALKED through the gate and into the courtyard. It was only a few hours before dawn, and they'd spent most of the night running around Rome, racing each other from one Christmas tree to the next and playing tag in the Piazza San Pietro like giddy children. More than one of Rome's numerous immortals saw them. None commented on their mad behavior.

Sometimes it was good to be a terribly feared monster.

Beatrice tilted her head and bit back a smile. "Wow. That's energy, Zeno."

"They're still...?" He tried not to laugh. "Indeed they are."

"I think it's been a long time for both of them."

He gave her his most pitiful expression. "For me as well, *tesoro*."

She calculated in her head. "Really? Ten hours?"

"Practically an eternity."

"That's what you get for not giving me presents in a timely fashion, you insatiable man."

He reached down and palmed his wife's firm backside, caressing one of his favorite personal landmarks. "I am insatiable. Are you complaining?"

"No," she said, tugging him into the house and running to

their room.

He tackled her just inside the door. Then, ignoring the faint cries of their guests' pleasure, he set about sating the hunger their playful romp through the city had aroused. After, when she lay boneless against his chest, he let his eyes close, content to slip into day rest as he felt the tiny pulls of the sun.

"Gio?"

"Hmm?"

"You never answered me the other day."

He frowned and opened his eyes. "About what?"

"What would you have done if I hadn't wanted to become immortal?"

The dark swept down. "Why do you ask this? It is a pointless question."

"I want to know."

He rolled away. "Beatrice—"

"Would you have left me when I got too old?"

He spun around, eyes wide. "What? No. Why would you even ask me that?"

She shrugged. "I just... I was thinking about Zeno and Fina. And Natalie too."

"I believe Natalie will turn when their children are old enough. Why are you asking me this?"

"Why won't you answer?"

Because the black memories fell over him. And they were heavy. So heavy.

"What do you want to hear?" he asked in a rough voice. "You want to hear that I would have watched you grow old? Raged silently at the loss of the one woman I have ever loved? That I would have counted the minutes and seconds of your life? Agonized over every stupid human way you could be killed?"

"Gio—"

"Do you want to know how I thought about it? Before you had decided on a life with me? When you were still mortal and *so* vulnerable? That often the darkness grew so black that I almost begged Tenzin to turn you *without your consent* because your fury would have been nothing to your death?"

"I'm sorry," she said, crawling to him and throwing her arms around his neck. "You're right. It was a stupid question. I'm sorry, Gio. I'm sorry."

She kept apologizing, but he stopped listening. He only wanted to hold her. Wanted to feel the strength of her arms. The touch of her *amnis* as her energy twined around his. He let his head fall on her shoulder.

She would be more powerful than him one day. The richness of her blood was evident, even in her youth. The thought did not threaten him. It reassured him.

"I would have loved you every minute I was allowed," he whispered. "And I hope you would have never known how much it hurt to lose you. I would have wanted only joy. Only peace. And when you were gone, I would have let myself burn. Because I have lived a long time, and the centuries would be too weary without you."

Her arms tightened around his neck. "Don't die, Gio. Don't ever leave me alone."

"Never." He pulled her head back to kiss her. "We are eternal."

ZENO NEEDED TO SEEK SHELTER, BUT HE DID NOT WANT TO leave Fina. She lay in his arms, naked and languid with pleasure. He'd exhausted her, and he did not feel the least bit sorry. He only wished they'd been in a more private location, because he wanted her sweet cries to fill the room. He wondered if the lightproof quarters in Perugia were sound-proofed as well.

A valid question before accepting a job offer.

"Zeno." She stretched out her legs, her toes tickling him. "Do you need to leave?"

He glanced at the clock. "I have time. Do you want me to go so you can sleep?"

She shook her head. "Tell me about your life."

"I know about my life; I'd rather hear about yours."

"You have more stories."

He chuckled. "I cannot argue with that. I was born in Naples."

"What year?"

"1893."

"Old man."

"But rather young for a vampire. My family was very common. Fishermen. And I wanted nothing to do with it. I had very grand aspirations and a very sound education actually. But I went to war."

"World War One?"

"Yes. I ran off to join as soon as I could. Stupid child. But I found that I was a rather good soldier." He smiled. "When the war was over, I also found the card skills I'd learned while I waited around for battle came in handy."

She lifted her head. "You were a gambler?"

"Yes, a successful one." He shook his head. "I made a lot of money. But after a time, the games, taking the money from boys and men who couldn't afford it, began to wear on me. It wasn't challenging. I turned my mind to business. Or what I called business. I loaned money to disreputable people, which was profitable but violent. I had money. Women. Automobiles and houses. But I could not go home. I would have shamed my mother."

"So you joined the church?"

"I hated it all. By the time I was thirty-five, I hated myself. I was cynical and angry. So I thought..." He shrugged. "I will give this all away. Give it to God. All of it. Even myself. Perhaps He could do something with this wreck of a man and his gains from so much suffering. It was impetuous, but I followed through with it. During the second war, it was a good place to be, even though Rome did not do enough." He clenched his teeth. "Not nearly enough. But still, I was able to move people who needed to be moved. Hide those who needed hiding."

"You were part of the resistance."

"The collar protected me. And the sisters." He grinned. "Never underestimate the fierce compassion of our Catholic sisters. There were many hidden in the convent who had never read a prayer book in their life. But they hid them. Many of them. And then... I became a vampire, but that is a story for another time. It was not as pleasant as joining the church."

She was looking at him with an awed expression. "You are a brave man, Zeno Ferrara."

"I don't know that I'm all that brave."

"Those who are not afraid of change are brave. And you have not only survived change, you have searched for it when life was not what you wanted. That is brave."

"Are you brave?"

She wrinkled her brow. "I don't know. I try to be."

"Cautious Fina."

"Caution is wisdom, isn't it? Life is unexpected. You have to be prepared for anything. I didn't expect to fall in love with my pig of a professor and become pregnant with Enzo, but I did. I was *not* cautious. And so I learned to be. And having my son was the best thing in my life. So unexpected!" A sweet smile crossed her lips. "I did not imagine my family would cut me off as they did, but I learned from it. And now

I am independent, not leaning on them for my security. And I'm happier for it. Yes, caution is wisdom."

"Not fear?"

She shook her head, and her quiet strength humbled him. "I don't think so, no."

"I think you are brave."

"I think you are very flattering."

"Am I allowed?"

"Yes, you are allowed." She rolled over and put her head on his chest. "Your heart beats."

"Sometimes, yes. Not always."

"And you did not bite me when we made love."

"Not this time, no."

"Where do you get your blood?"

"I drink mostly donated blood, but get it as fresh as I can. It loses potency for us the longer it is dead."

"Hmm." She frowned. "Did you not want to drink from me?"

He stroked over her head and down to her neck. "Oh yes. I want that very much."

"But you did not."

"I didn't want to scare you."

"Does it hurt?" she asked.

"Not unless I want it to. If I bit you, you would feel extreme pleasure."

She pursed her lips. "I think I have much to learn about vampires." Then she whispered, "Hands-on research might be necessary."

Zeno laughed as he twined a lock of her brown hair around his finger. "Do you know I could fall in love with you, Serafina Rossi?"

"That seems fair, since I feel the same way," she said, her eyes warming him even more than her body. "Life is quite unexpected, isn't it?"

Fina sat next to Zeno with Enzo on her other side. They had decided to attend the pope's midnight mass—which was actually a ten o'clock mass—on Christmas Eve. The tourists had poured into Rome, seemingly all at once. Flooding the markets and filling the streets, they spoke in every language imaginable, the lure of the Eternal City tempting people from all around the world.

But within the basilica, Fina felt peace spill over her. It was crowded, but Zeno had been able to acquire three tickets to sit inside the church. Ancient songs filled the air along with the smell of incense. Latin chants rang over myriad whispers in every language. She was reminded of her childhood, of Nonna's lace-covered head and scratchy Christmas dresses. The electric lights of Rome were beautiful, but it was the dripping candles near the altar that spoke of Christmas to her.

She felt Zeno tense beside her. "What is it?"

He leaned down to her ear. "There are many vampires here."

"Should we be concerned? I thought there were always many immortals in Rome."

"There are." He glanced over Fina's head to check Enzo, whose eyes were barely open.

"So why—"

"I did not have a woman and child before. I did not notice them as much."

She slipped her hand into his, and he gripped it. "You're going to be insufferably possessive for a while, aren't you?"

He grunted. "Possibly forever." Zeno's eyes narrowed on someone or something on the other side of the church. After several minutes, she felt him relax again. "Damn Catholic vampires," he muttered.

"Aren't you a Catholic vampire?"

"I'm young. Nostalgia is to be expected. The old ones cause me more concern."

"Shhh," she said, leaning into his side. "Listen."

The pope had started his address, his solemn voice filling the gold-clad-and-marble church. For hours, the crowd sat in silence, kneeling in prayer or listening to the beautiful songs that filled the air, occasionally intoning when the liturgy called for their response.

She clutched Zeno's hand, thinking about how much had changed over the years of his long life. And what had stayed the same. It made sense to her, despite his earlier complaint, that so many immortals clung to the traditions of the church. Whether they were devout or not, those traditions would be familiar.

The mass passed without vampire disruption despite Zeno's worries. It was only the three of them, as Giovanni and Beatrice had decided to celebrate at the Pantheon, which was near the house and did not attract as many tourists. As they filed out of the church, she felt Zeno's callused hand grip her own. Saw his arm drape over Enzo's shoulders as he guided them through the crowd. The mood was festive, but people were tired, ready to head to quiet homes and beds, and they found their way back to their neighborhood quite easily.

The previous days had been filled with sightseeing and shopping. Enzo, Angela, Rudy, and Fina had toured the city during the day and prepared the house for Christmas, always taking long afternoon naps so they could enjoy the night with their vampire hosts. Both nights, Zeno had joined them, earning some playful ribbing from Giovanni for his sudden disinterest in work.

But he *had* been working. She knew that when Zeno left her, deep in the night after hours of talking and loving, he returned to his cavernous workroom in the Vatican, searching for clues to the mystery of the disappearing Franciscan and his Antonia. Many of their whispered conversations were not the teasing exchanges of lovers but the polite—and sometimes contentious—debate of colleagues. And though she hadn't returned to the Vatican Library, Fina still felt a part of the research.

She loved it.

Zeno still had not bitten her, and Fina wondered whether it was her own hesitance that stopped him or if it was Zeno's struggle with his possessive nature that made him pause. He was, as Giovanni had teased her, a man of great passion. And energy. She'd never felt the complete focus of a lover as she did with Zeno. But still she wondered what would happen when she returned to Perugia and he remained in Rome.

"What are you stewing about, *cara?*"

"Hmm?" She looked up to see him watching her face with a frown. "I'm just tired. Don't glare."

"I'm not glaring."

Fina broke into a laugh. "You are a cranky old man, Zeno Ferrara."

"I am a dangerous creature, signorina. You would do well to remember." Despite the harsh words, his eyes laughed at her.

"How could I forget?" She shivered, and Zeno pulled her closer.

He *was* dangerous. She could see it lurking in the edges of his eyes at times, especially when they walked around the city. Could see it in the sweep of his eyes or the occasional way her hair stood on end when he was near. Sometimes she knew he sensed threats around them, but he was careful to shield her, even from the awareness of it.

Fina, knowing her own inexperience in the immortal world, did not press the issue. While she had no desire to live in ignorance, she also suspected that being with Zeno put her in the path of those who could harm her and her son without a second thought. She had no foolish desire to fight Zeno's protective instincts if he was keeping Enzo safe.

"What are you doing after you leave us?"

He lifted the corner of his mouth. "Who said I am leaving?"

"Aren't you going back to—"

"It's Christmas, Fina." He grinned. "Even my library is closed."

"Oh."

"Giovanni and Beatrice offered one of the lightproof rooms in their home," he said. "For the holiday."

She smiled as Enzo asked, "We'll see you on Christmas then, Zeno?"

"Yes. More Latin lessons tomorrow night." Zeno grinned. "No doubt Gio thinks I could use a review."

❧

BEATRICE TRIED NOT TO LET HER CHESHIRE GRIN SHOW

too much during Christmas dinner. After all, she was sure that, at some point, Zeno and Fina would have met without her machinations. Probably. It wouldn't have been as perfect as this though.

Fina and Enzo, charming single mother and son. Alone for so many years. Happy but incomplete. Zeno, a cranky loner who thought no one would understand him or welcome him. Two lonely people with uncommon interests, finding each other during a magical Christmas in Rome.

Oh yeah. She was good.

"You're looking very smug, *tesoro*." Gio lowered himself into the leather chair next to her.

"That's because I am. Very smug."

"I will admit they are well suited."

Beatrice snorted. "Please. They're perfect for each other. Has he given you an answer about Perugia yet?"

"Not yet. I wonder if he's asked Fina for her opinion. It would be a big change. And it seems fast."

"Fast? Kind of, yes. But they've been writing to each other for two years. So it doesn't seem that fast to me."

He shrugged. "I suppose you're correct."

Beatrice shook her head. "It's still so hard for you to admit that, isn't it?"

"Torturous." He leaned toward her. "Though... will you admit that I was correct to send Brother Pietro's letters to Perugia?"

Her mouth dropped open. "No! They belong—"

"Because if I had not..." His lips trailed up to her ear. "... who would have orchestrated such a perfect match, my love?"

"You're kind of evil."

"Admit you're glad I did it."

She mashed her lips together only to hear him laugh.

"Fine," she finally said. "Fine. Though you were

completely *wrong* to misfile my letters, the situation was salvaged by my stellar matchmaking skills."

"That's as much of a concession as I'm going to get, isn't it?"

"Yep."

"Fine. I suppose you're tired of arguing about the letters, aren't you?"

"It's Christmas." She leaned over and pressed a kiss to his cheek. "Even though it doesn't feel like it without presents. Let's not work."

"Presents come on Epiphany. I've told you."

"Whatever." She was still prepared to sulk. A little.

"So if we're not working," he started, "should I wait to tell you I've found Rafael and Antonia?"

"*What?*"

ఈంఆ

Fina tried to maintain her professional persona as they drove out of the city, staring out the windows of the hired car as city lights gave way to scattered houses. But she was excited. Never before had she participated in a search like this. Most of her career was spent in quiet offices and workrooms or searching online or through catalogs.

But this! She felt as if she were in a mystery novel.

"Excited?" Zeno asked, sitting next to her and watching her with the hint of a smile.

"Yes." She was buzzing.

He chuckled and pulled her hand into his lap.

The winery, a small family operation, was situated about one hundred kilometers from Rome in the hills outside Priverno. It was a small estate but an old one. The same family had owned it and farmed it for over two hundred years.

And Giovanni was positive it had been founded by the former Franciscan calling himself Rafael Szarka.

They pulled through the gates just after eight o'clock, the lights of the small tavern lit at the front of the house. The winery was on the same property as the house, with bare vines crawling up the hills dotted with oaks and olive trees. The tavern served the estate's wine, along with a small selection of dishes for those requiring a meal. Giovanni had called the night before, and the owner of the winery had been delighted to entertain a party from Rome, even at such a late hour.

As Fina stepped out of the car, she could see the signs of a building in decay. Though the vines they'd passed had been expertly tended and the rows spotless, the creeping evidence of poverty was all around. A broken border in the small garden. The sign hanging on a clumsily mended chain.

Villa Antonia.

"Signor Rosati, I must guess." Giovanni greeted the man who stepped out of the house.

"Yes, yes! Welcome. My wife has a dinner prepared for you with all the wine you would like. Come." The barrel-chested man held a hand toward the door of the stone-walled tavern. "We don't often get parties from Rome this time of year."

"Thank you for accommodating us," Fina said. "Everything smells delicious."

It did. And the table before them was loaded with traditional country fare. Cured meats and cheeses. Crusty breads and dried fruit. A stew of some kind sat in the center of the table, steam trickling from the sides of the heavy lid.

She gaped. Since she was the only one with a normal appetite, Fina wondered just how much she was going to have to eat in order not to offend their hosts.

"I hope you're hungry," Zeno said quietly.

73

"We should have brought Enzo."

"You're right. That boy would be able to swallow half the table in one sitting." He pulled out a chair for her and the four of them sat down.

"Signor Rosati," Beatrice said in softly accented Italian. "We were hoping you and your wife would join us for dinner."

The man pouring wine at the counter looked confused. "But—"

"We have a confession," Giovanni added with a charming smile. "We are not only tourists but historical researchers. Signor Ferrara, my friend, works for the Vatican Library in fact."

"Researchers?" Signora Rosati had joined her husband. "What are you researching?"

Fina said, "We'd like to know more about the history of the estate. We understand it has been in the same family for many years."

"Two hundred," Signor Rosati boomed. "My wife's family is very well-known for their vines. I was only lucky enough to marry her." He winked at Fina as he poured her glass.

Fina felt Zeno tense and put a hand on his knee. "Really?" she whispered.

"I'll get it under control."

She let him scoot closer and wondered if the possessiveness would eventually get annoying. For now it was amusing, and she hoped he'd be able to temper his instincts with time. She'd be more concerned if she didn't sense his own frustration.

"You are lucky my sister is visiting for the holidays," Signora Rosati said. "If you want to know about history, she is the one to ask. She keeps all the family papers and things like that."

Fina perked up. "She is visiting? Would she join us for dinner then? There is plenty to eat."

"And the wine will be far more enjoyable," Zeno said, "if we know more about it, signore."

More confused smiles and quick exchanges followed, but soon the two Rosatis and their sister, an older woman who introduced herself as Luisa, had joined them. Friendly conversation followed as food was served and wine flowed. Luckily, a very friendly spaniel had crawled under the table, and the three vampires with small appetites were able to smuggle her some of their food.

Fina wondered how the three other people didn't notice that vampires sat among them, chatting like common tourists. Their faces were fair, but the low tavern light hid Giovanni's pallor. Zeno, she presumed, had been more olive-skinned in life, which was his advantage as an immortal. Their movements were just a bit too quick to her eyes. Their teeth gleamed, and their eyes were too keen.

But then, she had ignored the prickling feeling that Lorenzo had induced. Ignored her instincts because no common explanation could be had. Humans simply did not look beyond the obvious unless they were forced to.

"So, Giovanni, Beatrice," Luisa asked, "what is it you are researching? The estate has many stories."

"We're curious about the founder," Beatrice said. "Who was he?"

Luisa grinned. "And you pick the most scandalous story! In fact, we did not know for many years what the truth was. There were rumors, of course. Because when our ancestor arrived in the region, he had no tie to it. No family or friends. He appeared with a pretty young wife and chest full of gold."

Zeno leaned an elbow on the table and sipped his wine. "Really? A chest full of gold?"

Luisa nodded. "That is the story. He bought the property and settled here. He'd brought some of his vines with him. Foreign vines, which was also scandalous to the locals, and he tended them himself. He had servants, but he worked with them. Not like a lord or a wealthy man at all. Rafael Szarka was a most unusual man for his time."

Fina said, "Szarka is not an Italian name."

"It's not." Luisa leaned forward, the delight evident on her face. "It is Hungarian. It was assumed by most of the town that he was *ungherese*, a Hungarian who had fled his homeland for some reason. But his wife, Antonia, was Italian. Though nobody knew from where."

"They married," Fina said. "They had a family."

Luisa cocked her head. "Oh yes. They had three children. Fifteen grandchildren. And after that the family spread. But always some stayed with the estate, taking care of the vines. Making the wine."

"It's a lovely story," Giovanni said. "But why did you call it a scandal?"

"Well, within the family there has always been some question of how Rafael ended up with that chest of gold. And where on earth he came from. Was he a noble bastard? A thief? Someone who had to flee in disgrace of a scandal? It has been the cause of many family stories, as you can imagine."

Signor Rosati said, "My vote was always that he was a pirate."

"And how would a pirate know how to make wine?" his wife asked with a laugh before she turned back to the table. "The mystery was solved only a few years ago. One of the old stone barns on the estate was falling down. It had been falling down for many years and only the children went to play on the rocks. But it was getting dangerous for the little ones. So some of my cousins and my husband went out and pulled it down. And when they were clearing away the rocks for a new wall, they found a chest of old papers and a few pieces of clothes. Very, very old."

"A sea chest!" Signor Rosati said. "I was so hopeful. But sadly... not a pirate."

"There was a journal though. In very good condition," Luisa said. "I was amazed. I was more amazed that it was written in Spanish and not Hungarian!"

Beatrice was practically jumping over the table. "Where is the journal now? What did you do with it?"

"I could not read it at all. It was in Spanish. *Old* Spanish. I took it to a history professor in Naples, where I work. He was fascinated of course. He asked to photograph it for his records and said he would offer a translation if he could publish an article about the manuscript. I said yes of course. He begged me to let him put it in the university library, but..."

Signora Rosati smiled. "It is our family history. It didn't seem right to give it away."

"The professor told me how to store it. Keep it well preserved. I have it in my home library," Luisa said.

Zeno asked, "And the translation?"

"The *scandalous* part. It turns out that Rafael Szarka was not a pirate but a *priest*. He'd run away from the church when he fell in love with Antonia. She was from a very prominent family but gave everything up to marry him."

"All the girls in the family loved that part," Signora Rosati said. "So romantic! He had traveled all the way from New Spain. From the missions in California. They came here under the name Szarka and stayed. In those days, of course, it would have been easy to change your name. They simply married and Antonia took his. There's no mention of her family ever bothering them."

Luisa said, "Much of the journal was about his life in California. Lots of technical information about wine cultivation."

"Quite interesting," Signor Rosati said. "We still use many of the pruning methods here in the vineyard that he did two hundred years ago. There are maps and diagrams of which vines grow best in different kinds of soil. Many things about grape cultivation that would have been very advanced for his time. It almost reads like a textbook."

"But with quite explicit notes in the margins," Luisa said with a grin. "There are other drawings other than vine diagrams. Rafael was quite an accomplished artist as well as a farmer. I have to assume he and Antonia knew each other rather *well* before he went to California. Or he had a very good imagination."

Beatrice said, "I somehow think he left those parts out of the copies he sent around to the Franciscans."

"Most likely," Giovanni said with a smile. "Poor Father Ignacio."

Luisa's ears perked up. "There are other copies?"

"We think so," Beatrice said. "We're not sure. We have a series of letters written between Rafael and Antonia's brother, who was also a priest. That is how we tracked down his name."

"Oh, I would love to see them."

Fina said, "I'll make sure to send you copies. The letters are in Rome right now."

"And you managed to find our ancestor from only some letters?" Signora Rosati asked. "That is amazing."

"We had a lot of help," Beatrice told her. "Signor Ferrara is a letter expert."

"I am," Zeno said with a decisive nod.

Fina bit back a smile. So modest, her vampire.

"Well... thank you so much!" Luisa said. "Thank you for finding us. We all think it's such a beautiful story. Are you going to write some kind of book or paper about them?"

"Actually..." Giovanni leaned his forearms on the table. "We have ulterior motives for searching you out."

Luisa said, "You want to examine Rafael's journal?"

"Of course," her sister said. "Perhaps take pictures for your research. I'm sure that will be fine."

"More than that," Giovanni said. "We have been authorized to make you an offer for the purchase of the journal. We are not only researchers, but we work as agents for very discreet collectors around the world. Collectors who, I assure you, make the preservation of manuscripts such as Rafael's one of their highest priorities."

Beatrice said, "Our client is a private individual with an interest in history relating to wine. He had heard of your ancestor's journal only through rumors. We were hired to find it and buy it for him. I can assure you it is for his own collection. And he will have no objection to the professor or your family keeping copies of the work. But he wants the original journal for his collection."

"Why?" Signor Rosati said. "It's unusual and interesting, but why would he want to buy it?"

"It is not my job to ask," Beatrice said, spreading her hands across the table. "I am only hired to find the book and broker the sale."

"But..." Luisa looked stricken. "We cannot sell it. It is our family history. We must—"

"How much?" Signora Rosati asked quietly.

Fina looked around the room again. It was a beautiful old room. A beautiful old house, built from the hill stones and weathered by time. But she could also see the signs of deterioration. This family could use the money.

Giovanni said, "Subject to our examination of the manuscript and its authentication, our client is prepared to offer you three million euros."

Jaws dropped around the table and an audible gasp was heard. Fina was flabbergasted. Early nineteenth-century journals, even rare ones, would be auctioned off for a fraction of that sum. Who on earth was their client? And why was he willing to pay so much?

Signora Rosati gripped her sister's hand, and Luisa nodded.

"Sold."

EPILOGUE

Los Angeles, California
One month later

The Hungarian sat down in Beatrice's private study, holding the precious journal with silk-gloved hands. He was a thin vampire with ascetic features and cold eyes. Beatrice had no idea how old he was, but his skin was extraordinarily pale, especially against his black hair and eyes. He paged through the journal as a man reads a book, a thin smile touching his lips occasionally as he traced the line of a drawing on the vellum.

The journal was remarkably intact, no doubt preserved by the sea chest it had been stowed in, which Beatrice had also been able to examine. The book was also very finely made, the vellum pages bound carefully and protected by a calfskin cover. The ink was faded, but the illustrations Rafael had wrought between the notes on grape cultivation were clear.

The Franciscan had been a gifted artist. Portraits of Antonia, drawn from memory, filled almost half the book. Often her curling hair entwined with tendrils of the vines he'd drawn on the page. There were also numerous landscapes and scenes of mission life, but the most detailed drawings were of his lover.

"We were fortunate that it was in such excellent condition," she said.

"It is as if I can see him writing the words on the pages even now," her client said softly. "Drawing her. How very strange."

"Were you his benefactor?"

He angled his head slightly, and she could see the lift of his brow. The Hungarian thought her impertinent. Oh well. Lots of older vampires did. Luckily, Beatrice's pedigree and connections—as well as her own reputation—protected her from most offense.

"His benefactor?" He looked back at the journal. "Of a sort."

"He returned to Europe a very wealthy man."

"Wealth is relative, of course. You say he married the woman."

"He did. They had three children and fifteen grandchildren. A very large extended family now. They still live on the estate and are far more comfortable after the sale of the journal."

The Hungarian closed the journal. "He would be pleased. Thank you, Ms. De Novo. Your work on this was excellent, and your fee will be transferred to your account within the hour."

"Of course." She rose and saw him to the entryway, the manuscript stored in the box she'd brought from Rome and carried by the human who had waited in the hall.

"Please give my regards to your mate." The client bowed with the old-world formality so many vampires preserved. "Perhaps the next time I am in America, we may meet."

"Of course. May I ask a question?"

"You may ask." He straightened the collar of his coat after Caspar helped him with it. Unspoken was the other half of the answer. *You can ask, but I probably won't answer.*

"Why?"

"Why did I want it?" He examined her with those painfully cold eyes. There was a flicker for only a second, then they were flat and emotionless again. "Sometimes, Ms. De Novo, a person can save a life without even realizing it."

"Did Rafael save yours?"

He paused, and the thin smile touched his lips for another second. Then he angled his head down in another slight bow. "Good night, Ms. De Novo. I'll send word if I have need of your services again."

❧

Rome, Italy
The following Christmas

THE SHOUTS OF LATIN VERBS AND A SKIDDING BALL mingled with laughter from the courtyard as Ben and Enzo tried to keep the ball away from Zeno, who had promised to remain at human speed for the duration of the game. Christmas in Rome that year wasn't nearly as low-key as it had been the last.

"I haven't had time to talk with you much," Beatrice said, sitting at the kitchen table next to Fina, who was cutting vegetables for dinner as Angela fussed over the stove.

"You haven't," the once-reserved librarian said with a smile. "What interesting book mysteries have you and Gio solved lately?"

"Nothing quite so fun as Rafael's journal."

"That *was* fun. I often wonder where it is now. Why your

client wanted it so much. I've enjoyed examining the digital copy."

"Don't let Zeno hear that." Beatrice smiled. "A *digital* copy? The horror."

Fina laughed. There was a flush in her cheeks. A quiet contentment that had added depth to her features.

"And how are things in Perugia?" Beatrice asked. "We're looking forward to our visit after New Year's."

"Things are going splendidly, though Zeno tried to appropriate an entire bookcase in the Greek section to keep magnifying glasses and dusting powders." She shook her head. "Incorrigible man."

Beatrice could easily imagine Zeno's temper butting up against the quiet determination of his partner. Fina would likely win every time, simply because Zeno didn't seem to be able to refuse her anything. They hadn't married or taken any traditional vows, but as far as she knew, the vampire and his human partner hadn't been separated for a single night since they officially met.

Zeno had moved to Perugia and taken residence in one of the lower rooms of the villa while Fina and Enzo remained in the house on the property. He'd bullied the administrators of the Vatican Library into letting him take many of his letters with him, arguing that no one else was really interested in his research and he'd bring them back eventually.

Beatrice was guessing they'd agreed just to get rid of him.

He had also taken on some of the responsibilities for the Vecchio Library, which Fina had been cautious, but eventually grateful, for him to assume. It allowed her greater freedom to explore how the library could be made more useful and which institutions were discreet and reputable enough to receive pieces on loan. Slowly she was revealing the library's riches to the world.

"Any decisions yet?" Beatrice asked.

Fina shook her head. "We have time. And Enzo is still young."

She knew the struggles both of them faced in their relationship. Knew that no one could make those decisions for them. She did know a quiet agreement had taken place between her husband and Zeno that if Fina did choose to become a vampire, Giovanni would act as her sire as Zeno could not.

Beatrice had a feeling that the love the two shared would only grow with time. And when her son was old enough, Fina would choose to give up the day for her lover. But life was unexpected, and no one could make that decision except Fina.

"It's good to have friends," Beatrice said. "Especially those who know what you're going through. Don't hesitate to call. Or even—don't tell Zeno—email me if you have a question."

Fina laughed and assured Beatrice she would. Then she took a glass of Antonia's wine out to her lover, who met her with an ardent kiss and a teasing smile. A vampire, yes. But also a man thoroughly in love.

Giovanni brushed a kiss on Beatrice's shoulder. "Merry Christmas, *tesoro*."

"Still no presents, Gio," she said with a sigh. "Not a single gift. Ben's going to back me up on this one."

He chuckled and pulled her to her feet. "Come with me."

"What? Why? I was helping Angela cook. Kind of." She allowed him to lead her up the stairs as Angela's laughter followed them.

He led them to their suite of rooms, which had been redecorated after the nightmare of Beatrice's first visit to Rome when Livia still ruled. Now it was filled with rich reds and blues, colors that were vivid even at night. Art hung all over the walls and—because it was their room—books were stacked everywhere. It wasn't the neatest place, but she loved it.

"Okay, what is it?" she asked.

"Come here." Giovanni put his hands over her eyes and guided her across the room. "I did get you a present, though it's also a present for me. And, being very unoriginal, I got the same present for Zeno and Fina."

"Wow, so I was thinking lingerie, but now I'm really hoping that's not what it is, because that would be weird."

"Agreed." He pulled away his hands. "Merry Christmas."

It wasn't lingerie. But it was perfect. A page from Rafael's journal had been reproduced on vellum, looking so much like the original that she had to check the edges of the drawing. Floating over a mat of wine-red linen, the page was a drawing of Antonia looking over her shoulder, her dark curls tumbling down and mingling with the grape vines drawn on the hillside. She smiled, and the look the artist had captured in her eyes perfectly matched the contentment that Beatrice had seen earlier in Fina.

"I thought they'd like a copy as well. To remember last Christmas. He really was an extraordinary artist, wasn't he?"

"It's perfect," she whispered, turning in his arms. "It's perfect, Gio."

"'She is all that is light and beauty in my life.'" Giovanni recited Rafael's words from his letter. "'My soul is but a mirror of her own. My heart, her twin in devotion. Surely God cannot condemn us. Surely the world must be kind. I will come for her, though oceans separate us. ... For what is an ocean against eternity?'"

"I love you."

"Merry Christmas."

THE END

DISCLAIMER

On behalf of all actual librarians, archivists, or other information technology professionals, I'd like to make it clear that real academic and historical research rarely, if ever, proceeds this quickly. Most of it takes months or years, but I didn't really have that much time in a Christmas novella. I just want to make it clear that *this is fiction*. (Then again, vampires who control the elements don't actually exist either, so you've probably guessed that I've taken a few liberties with the truth.)

Happy Holidays, everyone!

FINDING RICHARD

Giovanni Vecchio has a headache and Richard Montegu is it. Giovanni and Beatrice head east to New York City in order to take care of a little problem who's been spotted off-off-Broadway. They join Ben, Tenzin, Chloe, and Gavin to deal with a threat to the Elemental World. And a threat to Giovanni's sanity.

CHAPTER 1

Chloe leaned against Gavin's chest, enjoying the quiet peace of the bar as she paged through the latest theater openings. It was four thirty in the morning, the Dancing Bear had finally closed, and she needed to get to sleep, but she was debating whether to trek down to her room in SoHo at Ben and Tenzin's or stay at Gavin's slightly closer apartment.

Prudence said she needed to go home. Gavin's warm cologne and solid chest were trying to tell prudence to take a hike. He was humming under his breath and playing with a curl of her hair, seemingly content to act as her backrest while she read the paper.

Guest room. You're still staying in the guest room. There's nothing wrong with crashing at Gavin's.

If only her hormones were as calm as her internal voice.

Chloe settled her head against his shoulder and turned the page. There was a feature on the top left with the picture of a smiling cast in a new off-off-Broadway play that was starting to get some attention.

Imitation & Alchemy.

Chloe smiled. Catchy title.

She was about to turn the page when Gavin's hand came down on the paper. "What is that?" He pointed at the cast picture in the corner.

She yawned. "New play. Opened a couple of weeks ago way off-Broadway, but I've heard it's pretty good. Some stripped-down historical piece. Did you want to go?"

Gavin ignored her and brought the paper closer to his face. He narrowed his eyes and muttered, "You little bastard. Not this shit again."

Chloe frowned. "Do you know one of the actors?"

"What's he calling himself this time?" Gavin tugged the paper away from her and sat up straight, making Chloe lean forward in the booth.

"Gavin, what's wrong?"

He stood and walked to the bar, holding up a finger when Chloe began to protest. "One minute, darling." He picked up the old-style rotary phone on the corner of the bar. Most of their patrons thought it was for show.

It wasn't.

He held the phone up to his ear and then dialed numbers. "Giovanni." He paused. "Yes, she's fine." He glanced up at Chloe. "Wondering what the hell I'm banging on about, I'm sure. Listen..." He frowned. "Christmas? What are you talking about?"

"Christmas is next week," Chloe said. "He's probably wondering—"

"I'm staying here. Chloe is staying here. Yes, I've already bought her a present."

Chloe blinked. "You did?"

"We've got a problem," Gavin continued. "No, not that." He drummed his fingers on the bar. "Will you shut up? Thank you. That's not the problem. Or... that's not the problem that's currently in front of us. There's a new off-Broadway play in the paper."

"Off-off-Broadway," Chloe piped in. "Really, it's a tiny theater."

"No, it's not... Her first performance isn't until the spring. I'll send you tickets if you just shut up and listen." Gavin took a deep breath. "As much as I enjoy annoying you, I honestly hate to tell you... It's Richard."

CHAPTER 2

G iovanni took a deep breath and calmly hung up the phone. "That annoying little shit."

Beatrice raised her eyebrows at him. "And what has brought about this unusually spicy language tonight, my love?"

"Richard." He closed his eyes and shook his head. The last time Richard had been a problem, it had been in Japan in the mid-1980s.

Before that, it had been Norway in the 1960s.

Before that, Los Angeles.

Russia.

Buenos Aires.

Vienna.

Prague.

Why can't you just disappear like a well-behaved vampire?

"Who's Richard?" Beatrice asked.

"My own personal headache who could theoretically become every vampire's headache unless he grasps the last few remaining brain cells left in his head—which he won't—which makes him my own personal headache."

Beatrice reached for another puzzle piece in the five-thousand-piece monstrosity she'd spread over the library table. "That made almost zero sense. Why is he your personal headache, and why am I just now hearing about him?"

"Because I thought I made my point in 1983."

"When I was a year old," she muttered.

"Dear Lord." Giovanni laughed. "I really am a cradle robber."

"The worst." She looked up and winked at him. "But what happened in 1983?"

He stood and walked over to sit next to her. "Someone called me from Japan. A familiar face was starring in commercials. It was Richard."

She looked up. "Is Richard immortal?"

"Yes."

Her eyes went wide. "And he was starring in commercials? What on earth was he thinking? He's a vampire! And he was on-screen? Actually *in the commercials?*"

The headache was just getting worse. "Richard always manages to find a screen. Or a stage. Or... something."

Beatrice said, "Okay, I need way more information on this. And... why is he your headache again?"

Giovanni sighed. If only he'd kept his mouth shut.

If only...

༺༄༻

LONDON, 1863

The young vampire was sobbing in the corner of the room. As immortal beginnings went, it was... not promising.

Francis Winthrop, the vampire lord of London, was doing his best to offer the young man a friendly and encouraging perspective.

"Now, now, young friend," he said. "It's not as bad as all

that. Once you learn control, you'll be anything but a monster. Look at all of us. Do we look like monsters?"

The bright young man—whose blue eyes glistened with pink tears—looked around the room at Giovanni, Gemma, Terrance Ramsay, and Winthrop.

Giovanni realized Gemma, usually fastidious, had a slight smear of red blood at the corner of her mouth. He reached over to her with a linen handkerchief and dabbed it.

"Pardon me." She took the handkerchief and wiped the blood away. "Truly, Richard, I am so sorry I wasn't able to find the rogue before he killed you, but please stop whimpering and think of the bright side. He turned you into a vampire first!"

"Then you killed his maker," Ramsay muttered.

"Yes, I did," Gemma said with a fixed smile. "And if you'd heeded my warning when I spoke to you last month about that creature—"

"I can't kill an immortal because you have a vague feeling, *my lady*," Ramsay ground out in his thick accent. "Unlike your Italian friend, I'm not a mercenary. And in London, civilized vampire society—"

The brand-new vampire burst into tears again. He'd been bursting into tears every time any of them said the word *vampire*.

Giovanni ignored the mercenary dig. He had been a mercenary once, though it had been more than a century since he'd taken a client. Ramsay was new and clearly had his own ambitions to protect.

"Your life is not over." Winthrop soothed the young man. "Far from it, young Richard Montegu. You had a brilliant future ahead of you in the human world, and you'll still have a brilliant future. Just think! Your perfect face will never grow old. There won't be a wrinkle or a crease. Your body will remain ever-young. That golden hair will never fade or go grey."

The thought had clearly not occurred to the man yet. "I-it won't?" His mouth was clumsy around new fangs, but the resonance of his voice had only grown more golden. He would enchant others when he mastered it.

"No." Winthrop brushed Richard's hair gently. "You will remain as you are for eternity. You'll be just as beautiful in a century as you are right now. Isn't that good news?"

The young man began to smile. His smile dropped. He looked pensive. Then sad. Resolution began to arise within him. Every changing emotion was vivid in his expression. Giovanni could see the transformation behind his eyes.

The idea of immortality was growing on young Richard, and it looked like he might make the best of it.

"It *is* a shame you'll never act again," Giovanni said, flicking a piece of lint from his trousers. "You really were brilliant on the stage. That voice was created to play Hamlet."

Richard's expression swerved from heroic resolve to shock. Agony. *Tragedy*. His face crumpled, and this time his cries were loud enough to bring servants running. Gemma had to rush to the door to keep them from bursting in.

Ramsay turned to Giovanni. "What the actual fuck were you thinking, Vecchio?"

"What?" Giovanni shrugged. "It's true."

ॐ

WHAT THE ACTUAL FUCK WERE YOU THINKING, VECCHIO?

Ramsay's words had never rung truer. After a time, Richard Montegu mastered his vampiric instincts and took a very accommodating human lover who traveled with him. He found his fortune on stages across the continent, using different names and dodging in and out of human companies.

Rumors followed him, but humans were remarkably reluctant to believe anything other than the mundane, so Richard and his human companion—he always had a young and attractive one—escaped with their secrets intact.

But he grew bolder every year. And each time Richard came a little too close to revelation, someone would summon Giovanni—who was widely seen as responsible for Richard's delusions of grandeur—and Giovanni would have to take Richard by the proverbial scruff and drag him away from the spotlight.

Theaters across Europe. The early silent-film days in Los Angeles. The bright studio lights of Hollywood in the forties. The dark auteurs of Scandinavia in the sixties.

"Scandinavia?" Beatrice asked.

Giovanni grimaced. "Richard was obsessed with Bergman."

Then, most recently, Japanese commercials in the eighties.

"It's not the money," Giovanni explained. "Winthrop treated Richard as a son even though he was killed and turned by a rogue. He was a darling of London immortal society for decades. He has plenty of money."

"So what happened?"

"Francis was killed and it was horrible. Terry took over after that, and he had no particular affection for Richard, though to his credit, he gave Richard a solid portion of the inheritance, which he didn't have to do. But Terry never had the patience for the man. Wasn't impressed with his looks like Winthrop was. Because that is what Richard needs."

"Flattery?"

"Adulation." Giovanni sighed. "Attention. Admiration. Women and men—he doesn't care which—who just adore him."

"He sounds... really obnoxious; I'm not going to lie."

"He is... and he isn't. If you met him, you'd probably like

him. He absolutely brims with charm. And he really is an excellent actor. It's a shame he can't be onstage anymore, but I tried to make him understand the last time how permanent things are now. He can't just fake his death every ten or fifteen years and start a new life in the spotlight in another part of the globe."

"No. He really cannot."

"He has to be more careful. This is all going to catch up with him and then... it could get very bad."

"How bad?"

"He'll die." Giovanni looked up. "Someone will finally lose patience with his antics and they'll kill him, likely to prevent exposure of everyone else."

"And no one would blame them."

"Not a single vampire. Not even those who like Richard." Giovanni pressed his fingers to his temples. "I can't physically get headaches—I know I can't—but I'm fairly sure I have one."

"I'm sorry." Beatrice combed her fingers through his hair. "You do have a headache. His name is Richard."

CHAPTER 3

Ben leaned back in the narrow theater seat, his eyes trained on the stage below, which was lit with a single spotlight. The curtain was closed. Tenzin was next to him. Luckily, all performances of *Imitation & Alchemy* were after dark.

Which, knowing that a vampire played the lead, made perfect sense.

"At least Chloe says the play is good," he whispered.

"I don't like plays."

"You don't like confined spaces."

"You're correct, but I don't like plays in the park either. Why do people pay money to watch other people pretend to be people who don't exist?"

He took a second to parse that before he answered. "Sometimes actors play people who did exist."

She shook her head. "Historical inaccuracies are the rule. *Not* the exception. And plays are stupid."

"Plays are"—he turned to her, which was difficult in the tiny seats—"they're stories, Tenzin. It's a form of story-telling. They tell the audience a story. Sometimes it has a moral. Sometimes it's just funny. How do you not understand that?"

She gave him a blank look. "Then why don't they just have one person tell the story? Are human attention spans that short?"

Your attention span is that short. He didn't say it. It sounded petulant. "Just listen and try to spot the guy. Giovanni asked us to check it out."

"Fine." Tenzin plucked at the loose pants she wore. "I still want to see *Hamilton* though."

"Forget it," Ben said. "I'm taking Chloe. *You don't like plays,* remember?"

"It's a musical," Tenzin said. "That's completely different."

He opened his program. "I'm taking Chloe."

"She's already seen it!"

"Yes she has, and she'll enjoy seeing it again."

An older woman with crisp grey hair in the shape of a football helmet turned around and shushed them. Ben clamped a hand on Tenzin's knee and slapped a hand over her mouth just as Tenzin bared her fangs.

"Not here." He winced when she bit him. "Cut it out."

"I've been feeling hungry the past week." Tenzin glared at Helmet Head. "I believe she'll do nicely."

"She doesn't look like she'd taste very good," he whispered.

"It would be a spite-feeding."

A spite-feeding?

Ben had nothing to say to that. With Tenzin, sometimes it was easier to simply ignore her and hope she forgot she was irritated with someone.

"The *Hamilton* discussion is not over, by the way." She leaned closer as the curtains opened. "Just in case you think I forgot."

Ben turned, his lips an inch from Tenzin's. "Shhh."

She narrowed her eyes, but her mouth had turned up in the corner.

Watch the play, Ben mouthed.

The stage was noticeably blank. It was a historical piece, but in a theater this small, elaborate staging was impossible. Despite the size of the theater, every seat Ben could see was full.

The first actor came on, a woman dressed in servant's clothes, sweeping what looked like an old laboratory. A man emerged from the darkness behind her.

He was nearly incandescent in his beauty. Ben wasn't much for admiring men, but even he had to admit the actor was stunningly attractive. His hair was gold in the spotlight. His eyes, even from the back of the theater, were vivid blue. He had even features that would probably be described as patrician. He looked... noble.

And he was definitely a vampire.

"Oh!" The actress stopped sweeping and put a hand on her chest. "Sir, I am so sorry. I did not see you were in your laboratory. I would never have disturbed the great Comte de Saint Germain if I had known you were here."

"Please. I am only a humble alchemist."

A smattering of applause from the audience while Tenzin let out a loud cackle.

"Saint Germain?" She laughed. "He wasn't nearly that handsome."

Ben squeezed Tenzin's knee and offered a tight smile to Helmet Head, who'd turned around again. *Sorry*, he mouthed.

"Tenzin," he hissed in her ear. "You have to be quieter."

"Fine." She sulked. "But seriously—"

"Shhhhhhh."

This time Ben couldn't stop Tenzin before she bared her fangs.

Helmet Head, far from screaming in fright, rolled her

eyes, muttered something about "theater people" under her breath, and turned back to the stage.

Ben kept his hand on Tenzin through the performance, though he noticed that halfway through the first act, she'd stopped muttering about historical inaccuracies under her breath and was riveted to the performance.

"Do you see it?" she whispered at intermission.

"What?" Ben glanced around. Most of the audience was milling around in the aisle or had stepped outside for a smoke or a drink. "It's really good. I wanted to find it ridiculous, but it's not. The writing is good and the acting is way better than I'd expected. How much of this is true? Was he really— You know what? I don't want to know. I like the play. What are you talking about?"

"It's not the acting." Her eyes were lit up. "I mean, yes, it's better than I expected too, but that's not what I'm talking about."

"What then?" Ben frowned. "Did you really know this guy? Okay, I do want to know. Was he for real or—"

"Oh. Vampire. Totally. I think Saint Germain is living in South America somewhere this century. But that's not what I'm talking about."

Ben paged through the program again. "The guy who plays the count is definitely a vampire. He didn't even change his name much. Is he nuts? Richard Montez is not that far from Richard Montegu, which was his name in England according to—"

"They're all vampires."

Ben frowned. "No, they're not."

Tenzin gave him an incredulous look. "Yes. They are. Over half of them. And I'm betting the other half have fang marks somewhere on their body."

He blinked. "Oh."

"The makeup is good. Better than it usually is, but they're professionals. They know how to look human."

"Oh." Ben thought about the implications. "Oh. Oh... *shit*."

"Yes." Tenzin settled back in her seat. "Giovanni has far more than one headache this time. This time Richard has people."

Ben let out a long breath. "Fucking Richard."

"Great title for the play though."

He shook his head. "Something about this seems so surreal."

"More surreal than your life in general?"

"Good point."

CHAPTER 4

Giovanni tapped his foot in the back of the theater. A week after Ben had gone to see Richard's play, and now he and his wife were seeing it too.

Ben was right. The boy usually was, though Giovanni didn't tell him that. His nephew's ego was healthy enough as it was. But in this case, Ben was definitely right.

Richard was brilliant.

If life were different, he would be celebrated around the world. It wasn't simply looks. He had charisma. Charm. The innate ability to connect with audiences and find the humanity in every moment he performed. When he was speaking, it was nearly impossible to take your eyes off him.

Beatrice leaned over. "This play is really good."

"I know."

"What are you going to—"

"I have no idea." Giovanni felt his fangs grow long when a man in front of them turned and hushed them.

Beatrice placed her hand on his knee. "Don't. You're not really angry with him."

No, he was angry at that blasted vampire.

Dammit, Richard.

This time the actor hadn't only put himself at risk, he'd hired a whole crew of immortals and day people to back him up. Gavin and Chloe's discreet inquiries throughout the week led Giovanni to believe that this was a highly organized crew who weren't unknown, but they were discreet. All members of the cast had tacit permission to be in New York but were flying under the radar.

They were all here as tourists. Residents. Quiet immortals living their lives. Understood in that permission was the very sensible precaution to not stand in front of television recording cameras or up on stages. For immortals trying to live undetected among humans, these were commonsense precautions.

Precautions this acting troupe was flaunting shamelessly.

Giovanni could call Cormac O'Brien. He could end this in a moment.

But...

None of these vampires were hurting anyone. Gavin told him they were all well-controlled, nonviolent artistic types. None were wealthy, other than Richard, and Gavin suspected Richard was footing the bill for the production, though they were likely recouping their investment, judging by the audience numbers.

"He had to perform as Saint Germain," Giovanni muttered. "Of all the people."

Beatrice's smile was barely contained. "You have to admit, it's clever."

"It's dangerous."

"It's... meta?"

"I suppose that's one word for it."

"So I'm guessing we're waiting to meet the cast after the play?"

"Oh no. I have something far more cozy in mind."

THE DANCING BEAR WAS ONE OF GAVIN'S MORE AMUSING pubs. Giovanni's old friend had started pubs, bars, and clubs all over the world, usually spending a few years to establish the business before he "sold" the place to a holding company unassociated with his face and moved on to the next city.

Unlike *some* vampires, Gavin was extremely good at concealing who and what he was.

If human authorities wanted to look, it would appear that the "Wallace family" had spent several centuries quietly accumulating property and drinking establishments around the world. None of them would ever suspect anything supernatural was involved.

But this one in Hell's Kitchen exhibited a more whimsical side of Gavin that Giovanni almost found charming. Theater memorabilia of all kinds decorated the walls, from signed head shots and stunning costumes to carnival posters and burlesque revue masks. It was eclectic. Whimsical. And it was more telling about the state of his old friend's heart than any outward sign.

Chloe stood behind the bar, leaning toward Gavin and whispering something that brought a wry smile to the vampire's face.

Giovanni glanced at Beatrice, who was unamused. "Don't be a cynic."

"I've known that girl since she was fifteen."

"She's not fifteen anymore."

"And you think he's good enough for her?" Beatrice muttered. "*Gavin?*"

"I think..." He slid his arm around her waist. "I think it's none of our business. And Ben is far more protective of Chloe than even you are. So we need to stay out of it."

"I just want it noted that I have my reservations about

him and I'll be watching all this closely." Beatrice looked at the human and vampire couple. "Very closely."

Giovanni pulled her close. "Look at this place. Who do you think he built it for? For himself?" He looked around the room. "These are her people. Her friends. He built this place for her."

"He built it for the money."

"He can make money anywhere. He built this place for Chloe."

Though he couldn't deny the pub was a hive of activity. In Giovanni's experience, theater bars came with their own built-in entertainment. While a guitarist was playing in the corner, three patrons had stood to sing along with him. Several couples were dancing in the corner of the room, and actors in various levels of undress sat at tables around the room. It was three in the morning in New York, and the city's performers were finally entertaining themselves.

"Where are they?" Beatrice slipped her arm into Giovanni's.

"In the back room. Gavin says they reserved it for the company a week ago."

"And he only just discovered it was Richard?"

Giovanni shrugged. "He doesn't take care of special bookings. Chloe's job, and she had no idea they were immortal."

"And even if she did..."

"Vampires reserve rooms at Gavin's pubs regularly. His places are always considered neutral ground where they can..."

"Plot?"

"Or drink."

Drinking that wouldn't be quite so palatable to the humans in the rest of the bar. Giovanni pushed open the heavy wooden door to the party room, only to be blocked by a behemoth's chest.

"Private party." The accent was cockney, though the man looked Central Asian. Kazakh or Mongolian perhaps? He was part of the stage crew for the play. More importantly, he was a vampire and he was huge.

Giovanni glanced up. "My name is Giovanni Vecchio, formerly Giovanni Di Spada, son of Andros, son of Kato. Have you heard of me?"

The man's pale skin blanched. He nodded.

"Richard will be expecting me," Giovanni said quietly. "Allow me to pass."

"We don't want any trouble here," the man said more softly. "We're performers. We have permission from O'Brien—"

"Does O'Brien know what you're doing?" Giovanni asked. "Does he?"

From the vampire's silence, Giovanni knew Cormac had no idea that Richard had formed an all-vampire revue in the middle of Hell's Kitchen.

Beatrice spoke up. "We're here to help. If we can."

The guard nodded and stepped back.

The party behind him was in full swing. Richard was holding court at the end of a long table while vampires and their humans danced around him. Wine and blood wine was flowing. The scent of alcohol, sex, and blood filled the air.

Giovanni pushed through the crowd and stood quietly at Richard's shoulder, waiting for the vampire to notice him.

"My God, did you see them at the end tonight? I was half expecting panties with the roses," someone shouted.

"Richard, I swear if you wanted them, half the audience would have followed you home!"

"But do I want them to?" Richard winked. "Ask me tomorrow night."

"And the next," someone else shouted.

"And the next!" several more shouted.

"Is that so?" Giovanni said quietly.

Richard turned and the smile fell from his face. "Oh fuck."

⚜

"How does this continue to escape you?" Giovanni railed at him after the other vampires had been sent home. "You cannot do it, Richard. You cannot!"

The blond vampire sulked in the booth. The bar had closed and only Giovanni and Beatrice, Ben, Tenzin, Gavin, and Chloe remained. Ben and Chloe were behind the bar, quietly trying to polish glasses while the vampires in the room chastised one of their own.

Gavin said, "You risk us all, Richard."

Richard pointed at Gavin. "You were just fine making money off us when you didn't know who we were."

"Exactly. When I didn't know who you were." Gavin shook his head. "Do you honestly not see the problem with what you're doing?"

"You're just jealous of the attention we're getting."

"You have got to be joking," Gavin muttered. "You deal with him," he said to Giovanni before he walked away and sat at the bar near Chloe.

Giovanni stood ominously over Richard. "I could have called Cormac and this would have gone very differently," he said quietly. "I didn't do that because I don't want you hurt. I don't want your people hurt."

"They're good people harming no one."

"Do they know about you though? Do they know this is your practice? To make a mark in some place and leave others to clean up after you?"

"That is your interpretation, not mine. If you'd just let me—"

"I can't let you do anything!" Giovanni said. "It's frankly a miracle I haven't killed you yet. Not that I haven't been tempted, Richard."

Beatrice made a face. "I'm kind of tempted, to be honest."

"I'm not," Tenzin piped up. "I like you, Richard."

"Thank you, Tenzin!"

"But I wouldn't blame Giovanni for killing you if he wanted to. You're a pain in the ass."

Richard slumped down in the booth and sulked harder. "All we're trying to do is entertain you."

Giovanni scoffed. "To grab attention, you mean."

"No, it's not about the attention!"

Giovanni raised a doubtful eyebrow at Richard.

"Oh *fine*. It's about the attention for me. But it's not all about me."

"Of course it is."

"No, it's not! At least, not this time." Richard motioned toward the door. "Those vampires you sent home, they aren't mere immortals. They're *artists*. Actors. Writers. Costume makers. Makeup artists. Directors. They can't get work in a human company anymore." He turned to Gavin. "What would you do if you couldn't practice your business anymore? If you couldn't own a single bar? Business is your *art*." He looked at Chloe. "What if you couldn't dance?"

Chloe frowned. "How do you know I'm a dancer?"

"It's obvious, darling." Richard smiled. "The way you move—"

"Be very, very careful right now," Gavin muttered.

"—is very *graceful*." Richard turned to Giovanni. "What if you couldn't collect books? That's your art." He turned to Beatrice. "What would either of you do without your libraries and archives? They are your stage." He turned to Tenzin. "And what if you couldn't...?"

Tenzin smiled. "Kill people and steal things? You're right. That is my art."

Richard clearly didn't know what to say to that.

He turned back to Giovanni. "All this company wants is to practice their art. There's not a violent one among us."

"I don't doubt that," Gavin said, his accent growing stronger. "Just plenty of idiotic ones."

"I have no desire for harm to come to anyone," Giovanni said. "But you have to stop, Richard. You must. A video can spread around the world faster than Tenzin can fly now. What you're doing risks everything immortals have worked to hide since time began."

"And what then?" Richard said, his blue eyes welling with dramatic tears. "You say you don't want harm to come to us, but what of the harm of a crushed soul? What about the harm to our hearts when they long to tell the stories of the ages?" He stood. "What then, Giovanni Vecchio?"

For a moment, Giovanni was so moved by the agony on the man's face he forgot why he was chastising him. Then a slow clap from the bar broke the spell.

"Dude. For real, you're amazing," Ben said. "I almost forgot you're a professional liar."

"A professional liar?" Richard was aghast. Or... he was *acting* aghast.

It was really impossible to tell.

"Yeah." Ben walked from around the bar. "You're being an idiot, Dick. And don't pretend you're doing it for your friends. Who wrote this show?"

"I don't know what that has to do with anything, but his name is Joshua and he's an extremely gifted playwright."

"He is," Tenzin interjected. "I usually find plays very boring. His was not."

"But is Joshua starring in the lead?" Ben asked. "Is Joshua—"

"Joshua does not act and hates to be on stage," Richard said stiffly. "Geneva, his human, is his link to the world. This show pays for their life."

"And pays for yours," Ben said. "After all, you're taking most of the profit."

"Because I put up all the starting money. There is no guarantee a show will be a hit," Richard said. "The fact that this one is—"

"Makes it even more dangerous," Giovanni said. "Richard, I am somewhat convinced that your intentions *this time* are... noble"—*and self-serving*—"but the fact is, the company must stop. The nights you've already sold out can be played through, but after that, the show must stop. You must hide your face. You must. This isn't only for our protection, Richard. It's for your own."

Richard's expression was plaintive. "But Joshua—"

"Others can perform his plays," Gavin said. "You're not the only actor in the world."

"No." Richard's voice was defeated. He sat and looked at his feet, bitterness and resignation written all over his face. "I'm just the best."

The bar was silent for a long while.

"He's right." Chloe spoke up from behind the back of the room. "I know you're all right, but he is too. He's *really* good, and Richard, I don't know you, but I thought your play was amazing. I think you're right. You're probably the best actor on or off Broadway right now."

The actor brightened. "Thank you. If only that meant something in this cruel world."

Giovanni did not let his resolve weaken. This wasn't about Richard. This was about their entire world.

Chloe continued. "And I know I'm young and I don't really know much about the vampire world, but isn't there anything you can do? I mean... Patrons, I guess? Maybe? Is that a thing?"

Beatrice frowned. "What are you talking about?"

"Patrons?" Ben asked.

Her cheeks flushed rose under her light brown skin. "You know... patrons. Like in the old days when acting troupes and carnival people would travel around. Like in *Hamlet*. The actors showed up in court and the king gave them space to perform. And paid them. I mean, how many all-vampire acting troupes are there in the world? How many rich vampires are there? It just seems logical to me."

Brilliant girl. Giovanni glanced at Richard, who did not look hostile to the idea. He looked at Gavin, who was looking at Chloe.

He loves her.

Another thought for another time. Giovanni focused on Richard. "It's an idea, Richard. One that wouldn't end up with you meeting the sun or turning to dust."

"What kind of plays...?" He frowned. "Would anyone actually pay?"

"If we marketed it right," Gavin said quietly. "You should be like... Shakespeare. Like the greats. Performing for the highest vampire society. Play to those delusions of royalty and grandeur."

"I told you," Richard said, "it's not all about me this—"

"I'm talking about vampires, Dick." Gavin seemed to like Ben's nickname. "They like to pretend they're royalty. I could arrange to show your plays in the most exclusive venues—I have the connections—as long as you'd be willing to make it a traveling company."

"And pay you a percentage."

Gavin smiled. "That's the way the world works, Dick."

Richard mulled it over.

"It's a good idea," Giovanni said. "Vampires in charge of

cities would find the idea very desirable. It's entertainment for their people, and a way to show off how wealthy they are. If he was agreeable to it, your writer could even customize plays for the audience. Use the local lord's name for the king, for instance. Use the lady's name for the heroine. That kind of entertainment is the kind of thing immortals love spending money on."

Richard rose to his feet. "I could let Ermengarde and Victor open for me again."

"Ermengarde and Victor?" Ben asked.

"Brilliant gymnasts." Richard waved a dismissive hand. "You're too young to know them. But they are too obviously inhuman for human crowds. But for vampires, they could be our opening act. We could travel the world. Dine with the most glittering company."

"See?" Giovanni said. "Isn't that better than a human audience anyway? You'd have the adulation of immortals."

Richard ran to Chloe and kissed her hands before Gavin could protest. "You brilliant little human. Would you like to be my lover?"

"Fuck off, Dick," Gavin snapped.

"Uh... thanks?" Chloe's eyes were the size of saucers. "That's very flattering, but no. No, thank you."

"Your loss." Richard tossed his head and turned to the room. "We will fly, my friends. Fly higher and brighter than any acting company before us!"

Ben, Chloe, and Tenzin all broke into applause. Richard took a bow.

"And bloodier," Beatrice whispered.

Giovanni frowned. "What?"

"Bloodier than any other acting company before them. I'm just saying. Don't think I want to hang with their groupies, you know?"

"Excellent point."

"I'm full of 'em."

"You're full of it?" Giovanni pulled her to his side. "I'm hardly surprised."

"Ha ha ha."

Richard and Gavin put their heads together. Gavin must have thought he could make a good deal of money off the venture, otherwise he'd have twisted Richard's neck off for propositioning Chloe.

Ben was trading wry barbs with Tenzin in the opposite booth, and Chloe had picked up the rotary phone on the corner of the bar.

Giovanni watched the hum of activity and wondered if this was the last time he'd ever be called to deal with the problem that was Richard.

He probably wasn't that lucky.

CHAPTER 5

R ichard Montegu finally took his bows after the most brilliant performance of *Hamlet* Chloe had ever seen. She wasn't the biggest Shakespeare fan, but the first official production of the Saint Germain Players had to be in the top five theatrical experiences she'd ever witnessed.

And that was counting *Hamilton*.

The modern staging, setting the action within a film studio in the nineteen forties, was a stroke of brilliance that let the natural flamboyance of the cast shine. It was odd to see vampires on stage playing humans without the facade of being humans.

Of course, some of them *were* humans.

And there was a vampire movie being performed as the play within the play.

If Chloe thought about it too hard, she ended up with a headache.

The audience stood and clapped, maybe not as outwardly enthusiastic as a human crowd, but just as in awe of the lead actor. Richard was, quite simply, born to be on the stage.

Richard had been spending more time at the Dancing Bear with Gavin since Gavin had become his partner in the venture. The elegant vampire was preening and flattering, alternately insecure and egotistical. He was attention hungry and incredibly vain.

So... he was exactly like most lead actors Chloe had ever met.

"What did you think?" Gavin leaned down to ask among the applause.

"That was a hell of a show," she said. "How many more nights here?"

Gavin had rented out a small private theater for the performance. The show was lavish and intimate. Tickets were considered a prize and sold on an invitation-only basis.

And they were very, very expensive.

"They'll be in New York two more weeks. Then the show is going to Los Angeles. Already sold out there. Then a short engagement in Chicago before it goes overseas."

"London?"

"And Paris." Gavin smiled. "And Rome. Vienna. Berlin. Istanbul."

"You're going to make quite a lot of money off this, aren't you?"

"Yes, I am." He looked at her. "Does my money bother you?"

Chloe thought about it. "No, because you work. I think if you had it and didn't work, it would bother me, but I see how hard you work and you earn every penny." She nodded at the stage. "Especially when you work with Richard."

"Fucking Richard," Gavin said. "At least this way, if he's giving me headaches, I can threaten to cut his wardrobe budget. That shuts him up very quickly. The man likes velvet a little too much."

"Cruel. And inventive."

"And don't forget." Gavin put his arm around Chloe as the lights went up and the theater began to empty. "If he gets too bad, I can always call Giovanni."

Fin

DESIRES OF THE HEART

What defines love? Who defines family?

With their nephew growing older every year, Giovanni and Beatrice return to Rome for the holidays, this time with a new vision for their future and the future of their family.

Some lives are destined for joy. Some for pain. Can Beatrice conquer her own insecurities to create a new future for a child born in war?

CHAPTER 1

Rome
Christmas

B en spun in a circle, trying to spot the next clue. "We do this every year."

"And every year it's fun." Tenzin swooped over his head, teasing him as she gripped the end of the string. "Just find it already. I already did. You're so slow."

"No, I'm human and I can't see in the dark."

Beatrice watched them with a smile on her face. Ben was a good sport, but he was in his midtwenties and hardly got excited about playing the string game anymore.

Tenzin on the other hand...

"Ha!" He bent down and used a knife to pry up the cobblestone beneath his feet. "Found it." He unrolled the small paper beneath the stone and frowned. "Shit. Tenzin, I'm going to need your help on this one."

"It's Mandarin," Beatrice called. "You should know those characters."

Ben gave her a dirty look. "If someone hadn't completely changed the rules—"

"The old rules were too easy." Giovanni handed Beatrice a glass of red wine and sat next to her by the fountain. "Latin riddles in the house had been played out. The courtyard is an entirely new game."

"With more flying," Tenzin said. "Which makes everything better."

While the rules of the game had become progressively harder as Ben aged, the basic idea had remained the same. Clues placed in odd locations, linked with a single string, creating a web that only crossed at one point.

For Tenzin, a delightful flying challenge.

For Ben, a game his aunt forced him to play every Christmas.

For Beatrice, a reminder of a family and a childhood that were quickly fading into the past.

Her heart hurt. "It's too much."

"What?" Giovanni frowned. "You didn't want—"

"It's not— It just doesn't feel right without her. And him. What am I doing?" She dashed tears from her eyes. "I make him play this every year, and I know he doesn't like it. He just plays it for me. And he didn't even know my dad."

"It's not only your father's memory, it's your own. And it's a tradition." He put his arm around her. "Traditions are important."

Beatrice couldn't talk around the lump in her throat.

"She's recovering extraordinarily well," he continued quietly. "Her doctor said it. She has so much to live for. Caspar is with her at every moment, and you know how tough he is."

"I also know the statistics."

Giovanni said nothing because he knew she was right.

"Women over eighty have three times the risk of death in

the first year after a hip break," she said. "Even if they're healthy."

"Isadora is not a statistic," Giovanni said. "She's your grandmother."

"And she's old." Beatrice's smile was brittle. "I knew that —I *know* that—but somehow..."

"You thought she was going to live forever because you are." He squeezed her hand. "I know."

"Do you think we're making a mistake?" She looked up with shining eyes. "About this? Is the timing wrong?"

"If Isadora hadn't broken her hip, you wouldn't even be questioning it." His voice hardened, grew hoarse. "We've been talking about this for over two years now. Talking with Arturo for months."

"I know."

"So why are you second-guessing yourself?"

"Because..."

Why *was* she second-guessing herself?

If anything, it might give her grandmother more reason to fight back to health, not that Isadora claimed the hip fracture was slowing her down.

She was still in Los Angeles, surrounded by her adoring husband, countless friends, immortal family, and adoring staff. Beatrice checked in with Matt and Dez daily. Their daughter Carina was six and the light of Isadora's life.

Beatrice whispered, "You know why."

Giovanni slid an arm around her. "You're on the precipice of losing someone you love to natural death," he whispered. "It's normal to doubt allowing yourself to love someone new, someone who may one day choose not to spend eternity with us."

Beatrice watched Ben. "I'm thirty-seven and he's the closest thing I have to a son. And the thought of losing him..."

It terrified her. Froze her completely.

"I don't know what to tell you." Giovanni kissed her temple, the beard he'd been growing out rough against her skin. "Except that I've experienced this before. The love and the loss. I can't tell you it's not painful, because it is. I've lost friends. Lovers. I'll lose Caspar one day."

"And yet you still adopted Ben."

"Because I know something you still have to learn. The love is worth the loss."

She nodded. She wouldn't trade one moment with Ben, not ever. Even though every year that passed only brought his mortal end closer.

Change your mind.

Ben laughed and held up the last rock. "Found it!"

Change your mind. Don't make us say goodbye.

Tenzin flew over and tied the string around the base of the fountain, following it back to where the strings met in the branches of an evergreen tree that was decorated for the holidays. "So did I!"

She held up a bright red silk pouch filled with a prize that Beatrice knew both Ben and Tenzin would love.

Spanish gold coins from the eighteenth century.

"Oh!" Tenzin clutched the purse to her breast. "Do I have to share?"

"Yes," Beatrice and Giovanni said together.

Beatrice's life was crazy. And beautiful. And full.

And it had room.

"So," Giovanni said. "Are you ready?"

"I'm ready."

CHAPTER 2

The office of Arturo Leon was in Vatican City. Oddly enough, though vampires weren't officially recognized by the Catholic Church, there were more working in the Vatican than in most secular governments. Vampires around the world identified with the continuity and tradition of the Catholic Church, and there was more than one immortal member of clergy.

It was Arturo's job to keep track of them.

Beatrice and Giovanni sat side by side in front of a large oak desk Giovanni guessed had been carved in the baroque period. It was a jarring addition to an otherwise spare office. Sleek filing cabinets and floor-to-ceiling bookcases took up most of the space in the room. Giovanni suspected the filing cabinets were as ruthlessly organized as Arturo's bookshelves.

Beatrice was scanning the bookshelves while they waited for the priest. "Alphabetized within subject matter."

"You mean they're not just for decoration?"

She gave him an eyebrow, and Giovanni smiled and took her hand.

"You're not nervous anymore," he said.

"No."

"Why?"

"I have faith." She smiled. "Faith that whatever is meant to happen will happen. He may have changed his mind. We weren't exactly the most doting parents to Ben."

Giovanni took a deep breath and let it out. "He's still alive, isn't he?"

"That may be setting the bar a little too low."

"He's never been arrested."

"Yes, he has. We just got him out. With bribery."

Giovanni frowned. "I'd forgotten about that."

"So, we may not have passed whatever mysterious standards the man has invented. Who knows?"

"Don't worry." Giovanni squeezed her hand. "I have faith too."

The man in question entered the room with a gust of wind from the hallway that smelled of candle smoke, incense, and printer ink. "Mr. Vecchio and Ms. De Novo. I do apologize for keeping you waiting."

"We haven't been waiting long," Beatrice said. "It's fine."

"Nevertheless." The trim Spaniard sat in his seat and arranged two files before him. "I dislike being late for appointments." He opened one file. "I have your file here."

"I'm sure you do," Giovanni said quietly.

Arturo shot him a hard look, but Giovanni only smiled mildly.

"You are both confirmed Catholics," the priest said.

"We are," Beatrice said. "And we were married in the church."

"After your civil marriage in Santiago."

"Correct."

"Why did you delay your church marriage?" he asked.

"None of your business," Giovanni said.

Both Arturo and Beatrice stared at him.

Giovanni reclined in the seat. "Why all the questions, Arturo? We both know that I've raised human children successfully to adulthood. I keep my people safe. I put their needs before my own when it is necessary. Those under my aegis do not come to harm. Beatrice has lived an exemplary human and immortal life, establishing allies around the globe and conducting herself with extraordinary restraint, even for a young vampire."

"Yes, she is young."

Giovanni raised an eyebrow. "Is that what this is about?"

Beatrice spoke up. "What are your concerns?"

Arturo folded his hands on the desk. "It is normal for vampires of your age, men and women, to desire children. The human need for progeny does not die when you become immortal. But are you prepared to take a child who is not your own? Who has no relation to you? Your own mother—"

"My own mother was an asshole, which is why I'm glad I was raised by my grandmother, who was a saint. And a very devout Catholic too, not that it matters." Beatrice's voice was angry but controlled. "And any child Giovanni and I adopted would have a relation to me. She or he would be my son or daughter. Family isn't defined only by blood. Not for me."

Arturo looked at her for a long time. He gave a quick nod. "Very well. Your recommendations are very extensive, which I'm sure you know. And some were... unexpected."

"Dear Lord, did Tenzin send you a letter?" Giovanni rubbed his temple. "I told her—"

"Not only she"—Arturo lifted a sheaf of papers stapled together—"but the entire court of Penglai Island also submitted letters on your behalf."

Giovanni didn't know whether to be touched or annoyed. He hadn't asked Tenzin for any help because he was somewhat afraid she'd decide to take vengeance on his behalf should something go wrong in the process.

Apparently she'd ignored him.

"I have to say, this child will have very extensive connections in the immortal world before she even knows what a vampire is," Arturo muttered, paging through the documents. "I have letters from Penglai, Los Angeles, Ireland of course, here in Rome—"

"Oh, for heaven's sake," Beatrice muttered. "Did she tell everyone?"

"Apparently."

"I'm going to kill her."

"You shouldn't," Arturo said. "This speaks well for you. Though we typically don't approve of vampires publicizing adoptions—makes the children a target, of course—in your case, your alliances are secure enough that it helps rather than harms your case for others to know this child will belong to you."

Giovanni's heart leapt. "Does that mean she's ours?"

"No." Arturo closed their file and opened another. "She belongs to God and herself. But I have spoken to the committee in charge of refugee resettlement, as well as the sisters who have been caring for the little girl since her guardian was lost, and they agree with me that with the proper human help—which it is clear you have from your letters of evidence—you will make excellent adoptive parents. Even with your... peculiar condition."

"She's ours." Beatrice breathed out, gripping Giovanni's hand.

"You will be monitored," the priest said. "There will be home visits overseen by the bishop in Los Angeles." Arturo shot Giovanni a look. "You will be expected to cooperate fully."

He tried not to roll his eyes. "Of course."

"And keep in mind, this child has dealt with trauma, some of which may not be evident for some time.

Though she's only eighteen months, she has lost three caregivers."

"Three?"

"Her parents were mathematics professors and members of the Syrian church. They fled Aleppo when the mother was pregnant. The father was killed in transit to Turkey, and the child was born in a refugee camp. The mother drowned on the boat crossing, and the child was saved by another mother on the boat. She cared for the little girl until they reached Italy, but the woman already had three children. Taking care of a fourth was impossible. The child was surrendered to the sisters six months ago. She'd become quite attached to the woman who was caring for her. She hasn't coped well."

"And she's been in the orphanage since?"

"All efforts to find living family have failed. With the current political situation, records are nearly impossible to find. Once things stabilize, more research might prove fruitful, but for the moment, no living relatives have been located, and we don't want to keep her in an institutional setting longer than necessary. She is an orphan."

Giovanni would find the rest of her family. If it was possible to find them and give the little girl a link to her lost parents, he would find it.

"Other adoptive parents were considered," Arturo admitted. "Human parents. But the child doesn't sleep well. She acts out. She is... strong willed."

"Good," Giovanni muttered. "And of course she acts out. Her life has been one long series of losses. She needs routine. Safety. Consistency."

"I didn't sleep well either," Beatrice said. "Not for a long time. I lost my father twice."

Arturo continued, "It was determined that parents with your peculiar condition might actually be better suited to caring for her."

"Because we can use amnis?" Giovanni asked.

"That may have been a consideration, yes. You also speak or are willing to learn her native language."

"Giovanni speaks Arabic fluently," Beatrice said. "And I'm nearly fluent. I'll continue to study."

A hint of softness flickered in Arturo's eyes. "I'm sure you will, Ms. De Novo." He closed the file on his desk. "Are you ready to meet her?"

"Her name," Giovanni said. "What is the little girl's name?"

"Sadia," Arturo said.

"Destined for joy," Giovanni said.

What kind of mother had so much faith that she gave her daughter such a name in the middle of a war? What kind of child could live through so much in such a short period of time?

Destined for joy.

Sadia, whatever might have come before you, you are *destined for joy.*

And you are destined for us.

CHAPTER 3

B eatrice didn't know how she was supposed to feel on the way to the orphanage in the suburbs outside Rome. It was the middle of the night, but Arturo had assured them the girl would be awake. They were going to pick Sadia up that night and take her home with them. One of the sisters— a woman Arturo had chosen—would be going with them for a week of transition. The paperwork was already in process. Giovanni had already called Angela, Ben, and Tenzin at the house.

To Beatrice, the whole process seemed like a race to the finish after a very long marathon. They'd first started talking about adoption when Ben had moved permanently to New York and the house felt too empty. They'd started the process with Arturo Leon a year before after consulting with Carwyn about children most in need.

And now it seemed like everything was happening at once.

"It's a little like giving birth I guess," Beatrice said, her hand gripping Giovanni's. "Lots of waiting, and then everything happens quickly at the end."

The sisters who were coordinating the care of orphans in the convent assured them that a quick transition with a single caregiver was the easiest in the long term. Sadia hadn't bonded with any of her caregivers. She'd resisted any attempts at a relationship with the sisters and generally played on her own.

Beatrice held the picture in Sadia's file, the twin portraits of her parents printed out from the university website, where they were still listed as working.

The woman who looked back at Beatrice had kind hazel eyes, light brown hair, and a soft smile. The man looked serious, but his dark beard and unruly mop of hair reminded Beatrice of Giovanni. He had smile lines in the corner of his eyes that told Beatrice the solemn man in the picture didn't always look so stern.

Did Beatrice look as kind as this woman? Her skin was pale and her hair was a natural dark chocolate brown. Her eyes were dark brown and her skin was naturally cool, though she used amnis to keep it a more human temperature.

"Are you nervous?" Giovanni asked.

"Yes."

"Why?"

"I want her to like me." Beatrice gave him a rueful laugh. "I'm going to be her mother, and I don't even know what that is."

"You do." He pulled her hand into his lap and enfolded it in both of his. "You will be a wonderful mother. Don't listen to your doubts. Listen to your heart."

"Are you worried?"

The corner of his mouth turned up. "Yes."

"Okay." That made her feel better.

They kept their hands linked while the gates of the convent swung open. Their car was waved toward a small parking lot near a gated play area surrounded by trees and what looked like a vegetable garden.

The car stopped and the driver opened Beatrice's door. A car seat had already been installed between them. The bench across from the car seat held a small bag with a blanket and a book. The sisters had told them it was better to wait for presents.

Keep things simple and calm. Too much excitement will only lead to tears.

Tears from Sadia or from Beatrice?

She didn't need to breathe, but she did anyway, pacing her breath to the smiling young woman who ushered them into a playroom near the garden. A low light was glowing in the corner of the room, and a woman sat next to a little girl on a sofa, holding a book as the little girl sucked her thumb and plucked at her eyelashes.

The child looked exhausted. She had round cheeks and dark curls, her hair clearly inherited from her father. But her eyes were her mother's, a soft greyish hazel that shone in the lamplight. When Beatrice and Giovanni entered the room, she glanced at them, then back at the book. Then she looked up again, shifted closer to the woman with the book, and kept her eyes fixed on them as they approached.

The woman waved them over, and Beatrice sat next to her. "Hello," she said with a soft Irish accent. "I'm Sister Joan. I'm a good friend of Father Arturo's. And this is Sadia."

"*Marhaba*, Sadia," Beatrice said. "I'm Beatrice."

"Ciao, Sadia," Giovanni said.

Sadia stared at Beatrice, and her little hand reached out and clutched the leg of the sister. Her cheeks plumped as she sucked her thumb, and her eyes were wide and glossy with exhaustion.

Giovanni sat on the floor in front of the little girl, leaning back against the sofa and peeking over the sister's lap to see the book with brightly colored farm animals on the pages.

"Sadia likes this book very much," Sister Joan said.

"Does she?"

"Perhaps you'd like to read it?" Joan handed the book to Beatrice, who angled the book so Sadia could see.

Sadia kicked at Giovanni's shoulder, but he ignored her, looking at the pictures in the book.

Sadia kicked again, but Giovanni still ignored her. He spoke quietly with Sister Joan, chatting about the night and how long it had been since the little girl ate dinner. What had she eaten? What foods did she like? What kind of toys and games?

Sadia kicked Giovanni again.

Giovanni placed a hand on Sadia's foot and said firmly in Arabic, "No, Sadia. It's not kind to kick others."

Sadia popped her thumb out of her mouth, gaped for a moment, then hit Giovanni's hand.

"No," he said again, very softly in Arabic. "Hitting hurts. You should not hit."

She tried to smack him again with her baby-soft hand, but Giovanni grabbed it. "No. No hitting." He quickly kissed the back of it, then let it go before he continued speaking quietly with Joan.

Sadia's eyes went wide. She put her thumb in her mouth again and scooted toward Giovanni, holding out her arms. Very casually, Giovanni stood, picked her up, and set Sadia on his lap. The nun stood and motioned for Beatrice to scoot over. The nun moved to the other side of Giovanni. Within Sadia's sight, but a little ways away. Sadia turned her head and watched the sister, but her eyes were soon drooping. So she turned her attention back to the book with the colorful pictures of farm animals.

Beatrice read in a soft voice and Giovanni held the little

girl, rocking her slightly on his lap. After a few minutes, Sadia gave a great sigh and turned her cheek to Giovanni's chest. She put her ear over his heart, and Giovanni began to hum.

Beatrice watched as the little girl's eyes began to grow heavy. Heavier. Her blinks grew longer and longer.

"Why don't we go now?" Sister Joan said. "Before she's completely asleep. We don't want Sadia to wonder how she got to her new home. And let's take the book; it's a favorite of hers."

"We're going to go home now, Sadia." Giovanni stood, holding the little girl in his arms.

Sadia began to struggle. She took her thumb out of her mouth and began to whine, reaching for the nun.

"Sister Joan is coming with us," Beatrice said.

"Would you like me to hold you?" The nun approached with her hands out, but Sadia turned her face away, hiding it in Giovanni's shoulder and hitting his shoulder with her left hand.

"You're going home now, Sadia," he said in Arabic, walking toward the door. "Your real home. Do you like to ride in cars?"

Sadia stopped hitting, lifted her head, and looked around, her wide eyes taking in everything. Beatrice walked behind her. Joan was in front of them, speaking softly in a soothing voice.

"...sure everything is going to be fine. Your speaking her language will be a huge help. I can tell you have an easy way with children. She's not your first?"

"No, I have two human sons. One adopted around Sadia's age and the other when he was older. They're both grown now. Sadia is my first daughter."

"Oh, how delightful. She's young, but she's very bright. Very aware."

"I can see that."

Beatrice watched Sadia. The little girl rested in Giovanni's arms, her chin on his shoulder and her thumb in her mouth. Her eyes were fixed on Beatrice.

Who do you think you are? they seemed to ask. *And what do you think you're doing?*

Sadia nodded off in the car, woke when they arrived back at the house, then lay in a semiawake state as Ben and Tenzin did their best not to make a fuss around her. For most of the night, she was utterly glued to Giovanni.

The baby had refused the car seat despite attempts at bribery. Eventually Sister Joan relented when Giovanni reminded her that his hold was probably more secure than every seat belt in the car should an accident happen.

She had stayed stuck to Giovanni through the drive. Had clung to him when they entered the house and refused every attempt at soothing from anyone else.

Eventually he used a little bit of amnis to send her into a deep sleep and laid her in the crib they'd set up in the room next to theirs. Ben and Sister Joan would stay in Sadia's room throughout the day, and Ben had access to Giovanni and Beatrice's room should they be needed. Giovanni was hoping she'd sleep until sunset since they'd blacked out the curtains in the little girl's room.

Giovanni watched Beatrice as she lay in their bed.

"She doesn't like me," Beatrice said.

"She doesn't know you."

"She likes you." Beatrice rolled over. "I'm glad. I'm not jealous. I promise I'm not. I'm just relieved she seems to have latched on to one of us."

Giovanni slid into bed beside her. "I suspect I remind her of her father. Same hair. Same beard. Same accent."

"Did she know her father?"

"She would have heard his voice maybe. Or maybe her mother showed her pictures. It's hard to say."

"Or maybe she just likes you and not me." Beatrice sighed. "At least she ate the bananas I cut for her."

"It's our first night. She doesn't seem to like anyone much right now. Which is to be expected. We've uprooted her again."

"She didn't like the orphanage," Beatrice said with a yawn.

"How can you tell?"

"It's obvious." Her eyes began to droop. "She didn't cry when she left. Her face never even turned to look at it."

Huh. She was right. It hadn't struck him at the time because he'd been so focused on the car seat argument with Sister Joan. "It's a properly run orphanage. I checked it out before we arrived. Excellent educational programs. Child psychologists in residence. Family units set up for children in residence."

"I'm sure it's fine, but it wasn't her home," Beatrice said, her eyelids falling. "She knew it wasn't her home."

We will be her home.

Though they had many houses around the globe, Beatrice and Giovanni had decided that for at least the first year, they would remain in Los Angeles with Sadia. Dez, Matt, and Carina were close by. Isadora and Caspar shared the house. Tenzin and Ben were in New York but could get to the West Coast with a day's notice. They had already secured an Arabic-speaking nanny for Sadia during the day. She'd come highly recommended by Matt and Dez, who had found her through their contacts for employees of vampires.

"She's going to love you," Giovanni whispered to Beatrice. "She's going to fall in love with your laugh and your smile. Just like I did. She's going to learn to rely on your fierce protection and depend on your generous heart." He kissed her temple. "She doesn't know it yet, but she is destined for joy, and you're going to show it to her." Giovanni closed his eyes. "I know, because you showed it to me."

F our days after Sadia had come to the house in Rome, Sister Joan began to hang back taking care of her. She sat at the table, but she didn't feed the baby. She talked with Giovanni, Beatrice, and Benjamin, but she didn't intervene when Sadia got upset with any of them.

And she got upset a lot. Sometimes with Giovanni, but mostly with Beatrice. She was an utter and completely grump with Beatrice.

Beatrice didn't cut Sadia's food the right way, and the baby threw it on the ground. She didn't like the clothes that Beatrice picked out and turned into a tiny wild thing when Beatrice tried to get her dressed. She only fell asleep with Giovanni. She only smiled at Ben.

Beatrice felt like so much chopped liver.

Ben was having a joy of a time playing big brother, and just like Giovanni, Sadia seemed to have latched on to him.

"I shouldn't have expected anything else," Beatrice said, sitting next to Tenzin while Ben shook the ornaments on the Christmas tree, making the baby giggle. "They're two of the most charming men in the world. Of course she loves them."

Tenzin said, "But when she's hungry, she tugs on you."

"And then she throws the food at me. Should I be flattered?"

Tenzin cocked her head. "My daughter adored her father. Every time he was with her, she smiled and laughed. She was a very happy baby, but she laughed most with him."

Beatrice sat stunned. "You never talk about them."

"I had forgotten that memory." She shrugged. "I forget a lot. But girls love their fathers. That's very typical. They rely on their mothers. Just keep that in mind."

"I didn't rely on my mother," Beatrice said. "I did rely on my grandmother. So I guess there's that."

"The warmth and affection will come in time with her. The fact that she seems capable of it is a miracle. She's a wounded child, but she's doing incredibly well."

"We'll have setbacks. We've been warned."

"Of course you will."

"And she could need therapy for attachment disorders as she grows up."

Maybe Beatrice would too, because as much as she was devoted to Sadia's well-being, the flood of love and affection sure hadn't found her yet.

"And if she does need therapy, you'll get her what she needs." Tenzin bumped Beatrice's shoulder. "You're her mother."

You're her mother.

It didn't feel like it most of the time. Beatrice wondered if there was something permanently wrong with her because she didn't feel an overwhelming rush of love for the little grump. She worried. She watched.

But the love she'd expected to feel never came. The worry and the fear were all she had to keep her company as Sadia, Giovanni, and Ben seemed to grow closer every day.

The week came and went. Sadia barely seemed to notice

when Sister Joan said goodbye. The cheerful and encouraging nun gave Beatrice her phone number and told her to call with updates and any concerns. Beatrice smiled and thanked her for helping.

And that was that.

Sadia quickly fell into a nightly routine of Giovanni's making. She rose and ate breakfast in the afternoon with Ben and Angela. She took a short nap just before nightfall and woke, ready to explore with Giovanni. Books were clearly a favorite, but stuffed animals had also proven to be a hit.

The doll Beatrice gave her was not.

She had no interest in movies, but she loved seeing pictures on Ben's phone, especially short video clips of laughing or playing babies.

She was cross with Beatrice. The food still ended up on the floor and the cup was smacked across the table. She squirmed away from Beatrice's arms and threw books on the floor when Beatrice tried to read them.

More than once Beatrice had to hide in her room so no one would see the tears that threatened to choke her.

Who do you think you are?
What do you think you're doing?

CHAPTER 6

On the night before Christmas, Beatrice heard shrieking outside. She ran out to see Tenzin with Sadia in her arms, flying in circles around the courtyard.

Terror swamped her. "What are you doing?" she yelled.

Sadia's shrieks turned to peals of laughter. She was nearly choking with it.

"Tenzin, get down right now!"

"What?"

"Down! Now!"

"Fine." Tenzin landed and set Sadia on the ground. "She was having fun."

"She's eighteen months!"

"I wouldn't have dropped her. Do you think I would have dropped her? I did the same with Carina at that age. She loved it."

Sadia's laughter stopped and the little girl looked slightly green around the edges. She opened her mouth in a wail before she puked. Mashed banana and cereal came in a flood from the little girl's mouth, and she began to cry.

Beatrice pointed to the puke. "You are so totally cleaning that up."

Tenzin cocked her head. "I suppose it's a good thing we landed before that happened."

"Ya think?"

Sadia was still crying, her little face scrunched up in agony. Beatrice picked her up, ignoring the girl's stiff little spine, and marched her into the kitchen. The little grump was too miserable to shove Beatrice away. She shook with hiccups and heaves. Beatrice was fairly sure there was a trail of puke between the courtyard and the kitchen sink.

Tenzin could clean that up too.

Beatrice stood Sadia in the large farmhouse sink in Angela's kitchen, turning the water on and making sure it was warm before she stripped Sadia's shirt and pants off. They were covered in puke. The little girl began to shiver, and Beatrice tried to soothe her.

"Shhhh, baby. It's okay." She forgot to speak Arabic. She couldn't think of it in that moment when the girl was shaking and crying and clearly miserable. "It's okay, Sadia. You just got a little sick, didn't you? It's okay."

The little girl stood naked in the sink while Beatrice wet a washcloth and began rinsing her off. Her lip stuck out and her beautiful hazel eyes were full of tears.

"You'll be all clean in a minute." Beatrice rinsed her off and reached for the towel Angela had laid on the counter. "Should we get some milk for you? Why don't we get some new clothes and Angie can pour you some milk? That will feel good in your stomach."

Beatrice did everything by rote. She was Carina's favorite aunt and usually the one who ended up bandaging boo-boos since she was often the one who had helped the little girl get them in the first place. She'd helped Carina learn to ride a bike and jumped with her on the trampoline. She'd cleaned up her share of puke from the trampoline, that was for sure. She also climbed trees and taught Carina to swim.

Sadia watched Beatrice with wide eyes. They went to Sadia's room, and the little girl didn't protest when Beatrice picked out a soft green shirt and pair of knit pants. She let Beatrice pick her up and bring her back to the kitchen where Angie heated the little girl a cup of warm milk.

Then Beatrice took Sadia to the living room and put on an old American Christmas movie with talking reindeer and Santa Claus. She sat the baby on the sofa and turned to find a blanket to wrap her in. The night had grown cold, and Beatrice's elemental instincts were clamoring. She could feel rain coming.

She heard Sadia whining and turned around. "What is it?"

The little girl stuck out her lower lip and hit the space on the sofa next to her. "Mama."

Beatrice's stomach dropped. "What?"

"*Mama*," Sadia yelled and smacked the sofa.

Was she asking for her mother? What...?

"Mama!"

Beatrice walked over and Sadia pulled her arm until Beatrice sat next to her. Beatrice spread the blanket over her lap and over Sadia's shoulders.

Oh.

Ohhhh.

The little girl let out a deep sigh, leaned against Beatrice, and stuck her thumb in her mouth. She rested against Beatrice's leg and watched elves and reindeer and round men in red hats while Beatrice gaped at her.

That was it. That was all it took.

In that moment, Beatrice fell head over heels, crazy in love with the little grumpy girl who couldn't stand her one moment and might have just been calling her mama the next.

Who do you think you are?

What do you think you're doing?

"I *am* your mama," Beatrice whispered, stroking the curls back from Sadia's forehead. "Do you understand, Sadia? I am. And I promise I will be anything you need."

That night when Sadia felt sleepy, it was Beatrice she toddled to. It was Beatrice who rocked her in front of the fireplace and got her to fall asleep, and it was Beatrice who felt the soft press of Sadia's round cheek against her chest.

CHAPTER 7

Giovanni watched his wife on Christmas night, watched her delight seeing the newest member of their family tear through paper, open colorful boxes, and stick ribbons on Ben's head. Sadia tore each piece of paper on her present individually, then walked the piece over to Beatrice, set it in her lap, and waited for Beatrice to say, "Oh thank you, Sadia" before she returned to the tree to tear again.

Every gift had proceeded in the same way, whether that gift was for Sadia, Ben, Tenzin, or Angie. No one wanted to say no to her.

Yes, that will become a problem.

There would be many problems, many challenges, to come. Giovanni didn't fool himself that this moment of peace meant their journey would be a smooth one.

But for now, with the glow of joy on his wife's face, the warmth of the holiday filling the air, and the chime of Sadia's happy laugh when she tore into each present, he said nothing.

He was too happy.

Watching Beatrice's heart grow was the greatest gift he could imagine. Greater than gold or rare books or art.

Greater than any gift he'd experienced in over five hundred years of life. She was a beautiful mother, just as he'd known she would be.

And Sadia was a fighter. A survivor.

Giovanni could already see the will in her. Far from making him nervous, that will gave him comfort. Because their world was no place for the weak. Sadia would be protected. She would be watched. Giovanni would put a veritable fortress around her if he needed to.

But one day she would need that will, need that stubbornness, and need the survival instincts that had kept her personality whole through the trauma of her early life.

Others would call her difficult. Giovanni would call her strong.

And he would call her his.

The phone rang on the desk behind him. He went to answer it and heard a familiar voice on the other end of the line.

"Arturo tells me you have a daughter," Carwyn said.

"Yes." Giovanni smiled. "I have a daughter."

THE END

AFTERWORD

Dear Readers,

I hope you've enjoyed this re-release of *Lost Letters and Christmas Lights*, along with the newest short stories in the Elemental Mysteries series. While some stories and characters may be familiar to you, others might be new. I hope you'll read more about Ben, Tenzin, Gavin, and Chloe in the next Elemental Legacy book, *Blood Apprentice*, out this winter wherever books are sold. I've included a very special sneak preview of *Blood Apprentice* on the next page. I hope you'll check it out.

꧁꧂

I always love revisiting Giovanni and Beatrice, especially around the holidays, and I also hope you'll see with the newest addition of their family in *Desires of the Heart*, that you'll be hearing more from them in the future, even if it's just a short story every now and then. They'll also be showing up in Ben and Tenzin's series.

Thank you for making this series a forever favorite of mine. Thanks for loving these characters so much. I hope your holiday season is filled with joy, humor, and that you also find the desires of your heart.

I wish you all a blessed season and a happy new year.

With all my sincere thanks,
Elizabeth Hunter

PREVIEW: BLOOD APPRENTICE

৩৫৪

Ben Vecchio was a thief.

Tenzin swung the saber diagonally, but the thief blocked her with his own blade, a Japanese-forged katana she'd trained him on.

"You're insane," Ben shouted. "I didn't eat your cannoli."

"Then where is it, Ben?" She parried, forcing him to back up. "Did it just disappear? Did a mouse break into the refrigerator?"

A pink box that contained two cannoli and one cheese danish had occupied the refrigerator the night before. She'd risen from her meditation at nightfall. The danish had survived, but both cannoli were gone.

Ben growled as he blocked her relentless blows. "I am not responsible for your food choices, woman."

Tenzin wasn't a woman. She was a vampire. She didn't survive solely on blood, but she also didn't eat much.

She'd been waiting for the cannoli, and now it was gone.

He lunged right, tipping her off-balance and forcing her

across the training mat. The first floor of their apartment contained a large training area, various weapons, and oddly enough, dance equipment for their new roommate.

"I'm telling you, I had one. I don't know what happened to the other one. Why don't you just eat the danish if you're hungry?"

Tenzin's eyes went wide. "The danish isn't mine. The danish is Chloe's. The cannoli is mine. Only one person loves cannoli more than me in this house." She spun around the slapped the back of his thighs with the flat of her sword. "You didn't even get rid of the evidence. You're worse than a thief. You're a *bad* thief."

Ben's eyes narrowed. "Take it back."

"No."

He attacked. The room filled with the furious clashing blades of two enemies ignited by righteous fury. She forced herself to stay on the ground. Just because she could fly didn't mean she would. Not when it would only draw complaints about unfair advantages of being immortal.

Oh no. Tenzin wanted vengeance, and she didn't want to hear Ben whining about it.

Blood or no blood? She decided she didn't want to hear complaints from Chloe about cleaning up the training area, so she kept to slaps with the flat of her blade.

"You're a bad thief," she taunted him with a slap to the bicep. "Slow."

"Shut up." He slapped back and her ass felt it. "I'm the fastest human you know."

He was the fastest human she knew, but Tenzin wasn't going to admit it. Ben was a human in an immortal world, and he did everything possible to even the playing field.

He practiced and trained relentlessly, carving his tall, lean body into a weapon as flexible and lethal as a rapier. He mastered martial arts from South America and Asia. He'd studied knife fighting with masters. He'd killed his first enemy at sixteen in defense of a friend, matched wits with emperors, and bargained with ancients.

"If you're so fast, maybe you should have run out and gotten another cannoli instead of stealing mine." She darted to the side, just escaping the blade that would have slapped the back of her knee.

Close.

Tenzin narrowed her eyes. That was the closest he'd ever gotten without her allowing it.

She jumped into the air and flew over his head, kneeing him in the right kidney and quickly punching her knuckle into the nerve above his elbow.

Ben grunted and fumbled the blade. "Cheater."

"Thief."

He dropped his shoulder and flipped her over. "It is the height of hypocrisy for you to be calling *me* a thief!"

Tenzin hit the ground and Ben was on her, straddling her hips with his knees and twisting her wrist until she loosened her grip on the weapon she carried.

Did she notice how broad his shoulders had become? Perhaps. Did she notice how lean his hips were and how penetrating his gaze was? Yes. She'd have to be blind not to see what an attractive man he'd become.

He still made her irrationally angry. "That was my cannoli."

"Enough." His normally affable expression was gone. It had been gone for months.

"Why would you buy me a treat and then take it for yourself?" she asked. "That makes no sense."

"Because I didn't." He rolled off her and lay flat on the mat. "Don't pick up that fucking sword again, or I'm gonna lose my last nerve. I swear it."

She'd been hoping a good fight would perk him up, but it seemed to have only annoyed him. And his lip was bleeding.

Oops.

"What is wrong with you?" He pinched the arch of his nose. "Were you just bored? I was trying to wrap my brain around this fucking Bucharest job, and you're busting my balls about cannoli for fuck's sake."

"Is it wrong that I kind of like it when your New Yorker comes out?"

"What the fuck are you talking about?"

Tenzin couldn't stop the smile.

Ben stood up, reaching a hand out to help her up before he grabbed the katana and the dao they'd been fighting with, walked to the long racks at the edge of the training area, and put both weapons in their place. Then he grabbed a towel from the bench nearby.

Just one. Tenzin didn't sweat.

She crossed her arms over her chest. "The Bucharest job is vexing you because Radu hasn't given you all the information yet. You still don't know who his sire is, so you don't know if he has any siblings, so you don't know if anyone else has a claim on that icon. Until you find out if he's the only one with a claim, you're not going to feel comfortable bending the rules necessary for this job. Conscience, Ben. It's your greatest weakness."

"I'm so glad you think so," Ben muttered. "Radu's not going to tell me who his sire is."

"Then tell him you can't help him."

He wiped the towel across his forehead. "This would be our first job in Eastern Europe. And Radu knows every vampire between Prague and Tbilisi."

"Radu is a pain in the ass," Tenzin said. "Every vampire between Prague and Tbilisi knows Radu is a pain in the ass.

We're not going to lose face if we tell him we don't want the job."

"The finder's fee on this one is healthy. Giovanni encouraged me to say yes. He's not officially my boss..."

"But he's kind of your boss." The jobs that Tenzin and Ben took were closer to the art world than the historical world that Ben's adopted uncle, Giovanni Vecchio, had worked in for centuries. But the concept was the same. If you were an immortal who'd lost something, they could help you find it. Ancient Tibetan scroll? Giovanni was your man. Medieval Russian icon? That was Ben and Tenzin's department.

"Gio probably considers a job for Radu character-building," Tenzin said. "He's self-righteous like that."

"But is he right?"

"Maybe. Do you really need your character built more?"

"According to my uncle"—Ben raised a familiar eyebrow —"character is a construction of eternity, an endless striving of the self to be subsumed to the greater good."

Tenzin rolled her eyes, partly because Ben's imitation of her old friend was just that good. "Ancestors, save me from philosophers."

Ben almost cracked a smile. Almost. "Right now I'm more motivated by Radu's bank account."

"Like either of us needs the money." She eyed the new construction next to the training area. "But the money would be nice."

She could smell plaster dust in the air from the workmen who were finishing the bathroom attached to the new bedroom they'd added. Chloe had overseen the construction, just like she was now overseeing most human aspects of their business. She answered mail and ran errands. She kept track of various accounts and helped Ben move money when it was necessary.

Tenzin didn't need to move money from banks. She kept all her earnings in gold. She liked gold. Radu was offering to pay in gold.

"He's been missing that icon for a hundred and fifty years," Tenzin said. "And bitching about it for at least a century. You can push him off for a while. Send him something by courier and tell the courier to get lost. You can put him off for at least another year with that trick."

"Really?" Ben looked skeptical.

"Trust me. I've used it many times. Especially if my father summons me."

"Good to know."

She tilted her head back to look at him. "Did you eat that cannoli?"

Ben tapped her forehead. "Fucking one-track mind. No. I did not eat your cannoli. And I'm ending this conversation before it gets more ridiculous. I'm hungry. I'm going to make dinner."

"Fatoush?"

"I made that last night. Chloe is picking up some lamb. Figured I'd try making polo if you want."

"Well, if there's no cannoli..."

The edge of his mouth barely tilted up. "I'll make enough for three."

Tenzin followed Ben up the stairs. "You should put ice on that lip."

"Thanks for the tip." He peeled off his shirt, which was covered in sweat, and tossed it over his head, hitting her smack in the face.

Tenzin wrinkled her nose and held the shirt with two fingers. "But you should shower first. You stink."

"Yeah, I got ambushed before I could clean up. I wonder how that happened?"

"I consider cannoli theft between partners a serious

offense." They made it up the stairs, and Tenzin heard Chloe humming in the kitchen. "Hello, Chloe."

"Hey, guys!" The cheerful human—the only one in the house these days—waved at them. She must have just come from rehearsal because she was wearing leggings and a loose top. Her dark spirals of hair were pulled up into a giant pony-tail, and her light brown skin glowed with health. She'd made vast progress since she'd left her abusive boyfriend and moved in with them.

Tenzin was definitely going to keep her.

"Ben, the lamb you wanted is in the fridge." Chloe looked up. "What did you do to your lip?"

Ben turned and glared at Tenzin. "Ask Tiny."

"Sparring?" Chloe turned to the fridge. "Oh! Tenzin, before I forget. I ate that cannoli Ben brought home yesterday because a chocolate craving hit hard before rehearsal, but I got you another one from Masseria."

"Thank you." Tenzin walked to the fridge. Excellent. A fresh cannoli was even better than a day-old one, though Masseria's cannoli crust always held up well, even overnight.

Ben's mouth was open. "That's it?"

Tenzin opened the refrigerator and removed the pastry from the box before she answered. "What?" She took a bite and sighed in happiness.

Ben walked across the kitchen, slammed the refrigerator door shut, and towered over her. "You ambush me, give me a bloody lip and a bruise in my fucking hamstring because you think I took your cannoli, and Chloe waltzes in, admits to stealing the thing, and all she gets is an 'okay cool?'"

Tenzin held up the crusty pastry tube of deliciousness. "But she got me another one."

"Unbelievable." He stormed out of the kitchen and down the stairs. A few minutes later, Tenzin heard the water in the shower switch on.

Chloe pursed her lips. "He's so tense right now."

"I know. I keep trying to think of ways for him to relax, but nothing is working."

Chloe cut her eyes toward Tenzin. "I can think of one thing."

"Wrestling?"

"I suppose some people might call it that."

"You're right. He hasn't had a good jiujitsu match in ages. We should research facilities in the neighborhood. There have to be some options."

"Jiujitsu." Chloe smiled. "Sure. That's exactly what I was thinking."

"Yes, you're very smart for a human."

"Well, I'm glad one of us is."

Tenzin bit her lip to keep from laughing. She wasn't as clueless about the tension between her and Ben as they all liked to think.

She just didn't know what she wanted to do about it yet.

⚜️

He lived most of his life at night. He slept when the sun was at its zenith and came to life with the stars. If workmen filled the house, he sometimes took refuge in the library, sleeping in a dark corner on the pallet Tenzin used for meditating. When he was tired, he slept, and it could be anywhere in the loft that had become home to the strange little family of human, vampire, and whatever hybrid Ben had become.

He was in the library that night, searching for more information on a medieval Russian icon. Though Chloe had gone to sleep, Ben remained awake. He was lithe and silent, his body trained to move in ways that avoided attention. Tenzin watched him from her perch in the sheltered loft he'd designed with her in mind. It was sun safe no matter the hour of the day. It was plain but spacious. Most importantly, only Tenzin had access to it.

Though Ben occasionally dragged a ladder over if he was feeling ornery.

He wasn't particularly tall for a modern human, though he was far larger than Tenzin. His features were a blend of the blood that had made him, half from the Old World and half from the New. His human father had been Puerto Rican. His mother, Lebanese. The blood of every continent flowed in his veins.

But his eyes—those dark, watchful eyes—came from the vampire who had made him the man he was.

Ben moved silently in the library, opening one reference book after another, jumping between his laptop computer and the books. He was following a trail of some kind, slowly narrowing his search area.

He had become a fine hunter.

It was an odd thing, Tenzin thought as she watched him, to see the slow transformation of a novice. Ben had never been a child to her. She'd met him when he was a teenager who looked no older than she did, but he had never been a child. Life had taught him early that fate was not kind to the young.

While he remained human, he would grow older every year. Unlike Tenzin, whose face hadn't changed in five millennia, Ben's features became more rugged. His beard grew thicker. His expression more solemn.

While he remained human...

"I don't want it, Tiny. You know I don't. I'm too familiar with vampire life to idealize immortality."

He knew nothing.

"Promise me."

Tenzin had made many promises over the years. She'd broken most of them.

She spotted the map that he'd been avoiding for a year. It was sitting in a clear plastic sleeve on the edge of a bookshelf.

Tenzin cocked her head and thought about the map to the rumored treasure of the famed privateer Miguel Enríquez, about an island still ravaged by a hurricane, and about an old woman who carried Ben's last true link to the human world.

"I don't want it."

And yet...

He lived most of his life at night. He slept when the sun was at its zenith and came to life with the stars.

Are you truly human anymore, my Benjamin?

Tenzin flew down to him, grabbing the map from the bookshelf before she sat next to him on the table.

Ben looked up from his computer and spotted what she was holding. "Not this again."

"It's been a year."

His expression was carefully neutral. "And we only got a letter back from the island a couple of months ago."

"We didn't need to wait for a letter. You know that."

"We did. Giovanni—"

"This isn't about protocol, Benjamin." She put the map in front of him and bent down. "This isn't about appeasing the current vampire in charge of—"

"Three, actually. There are three vampires in charge of Puerto Rico."

She kept talking and ignored the way the Spanish name rolled off his tongue. Ben was annoyingly attractive when he spoke Spanish. "This is about you avoiding your past. Avoiding a place that might still have some hold on you."

"You think so?" His eyes were heated. "Don't pretend this is about me. I didn't take this map. I wanted nothing to do with it. You wanted to hunt pirate treasure, Tenzin. You didn't care what the island had been through or what conditions people were living in."

"Yes, I wanted to find the treasure. Other people are not my problem. The chaos directly after the hurricane would have cloaked our movements. And there was almost no electricity. You know I love that."

Ben closed his eyes. "Could you at least pretend to care?"

"Why? I thought this wasn't about your family, Ben. Why would I care about strangers?"

He had no answer for that.

"You care," she said. "And that's fine. Your caring doesn't bother me. Maybe when we go down, you can do more than send anonymous money to your grandmother. But all I care about is following this map and finding treasure. You are delaying for personal reasons that don't have anything to do with business."

He opened his eyes and glared at her. "Fine. You want to hunt pirate treasure, we'll hunt. But we're doing this in a respectful way, and we're not charging down there without an introduction."

."Excellent." She sat up. "Then you'll be happy to know I made a date for you and Novia to have drinks tomorrow night."

Why was Spanish so effective? She even found it attractive when he was cursing.

৬২৩

Blood Apprentice will be available in Winter 2018 at all major retailers in e-book, paperback, and audio.
For more information:
ElizabethHunterWrites.com

SIGN UP FOR A FREE SHORT STORY

Thank you for taking the time to read this book! If you enjoy a book, one of the best things you can do to support an author is to leave an honest review wherever you bought your copy. Thank you for taking the time to let others know what you thought.

Sign up for my newsletter today and receive a bonus short story "Too Many Cooks" FREE in your inbox! Subscribers receive monthly updates, new book alerts, exclusive contests, and original short fiction featuring favorite characters from my books.

ABOUT THE AUTHOR

ELIZABETH HUNTER is a *USA Today* and international best-selling author of romance, contemporary fantasy, and paranormal mystery. Based in Central California, she travels extensively to write fantasy fiction exploring world mythologies, history, and the universal bonds of love, friendship, and family. She has published over thirty works of fiction and sold over a million books worldwide. She is the author of Love Stories on 7th and Main, the Elemental Legacy series, the Irin Chronicles, the Cambio Springs Mysteries, and other works of fiction.

ElizabethHunterWrites.com

ALSO BY ELIZABETH HUNTER

The Elemental Mysteries

A Hidden Fire

This Same Earth

The Force of Wind

A Fall of Water

The Stars Afire

The Elemental World

Building From Ashes

Waterlocked (novella)

Blood and Sand

The Bronze Blade (novella)

The Scarlet Deep

Beneath a Waning Moon (novella)

A Stone-Kissed Sea

The Elemental Legacy

Shadows and Gold

Imitation and Alchemy

Omens and Artifacts

Midnight Labyrinth

Blood Apprentice (Winter 2019)

The Irin Chronicles

The Scribe

The Singer

The Secret

The Staff and the Blade

The Silent

The Storm

The Seeker

The Cambio Springs Series

Long Ride Home (short story)

Shifting Dreams

Five Mornings (short story)

Desert Bound

Waking Hearts

Contemporary Romance

The Genius and the Muse

7th and Main

INK

HOOKED (Winter 2019)

Linx & Bogie Mysteries

A Ghost in the Glamour

A Bogie in the Boat

Made in the USA
Monee, IL
12 July 2020